BROOM FLYER'S
TALES & SPELLS

a collection by
R. H. BURKETT

Executive Editor – Clarissa Willis
Publishing Coordinator – Sharon Kizziah-Holmes

SOLANDER
PRESS

Solander Press
Rogers Arkansas

ISBN -13: 978-1-959548-05-8

DEDICATION

To Winnie Watson Burkett

ACKNOWLEDGEMENTS

Thank you, Clarissa (Chrissy) Willis and Sharon Kizziah-Holmes, for your help and expertise with this project.

THE COWBOY AND PAINT

The Cowboy sat proud and tall in the saddle
Watching below his grazing cattle.
His horse moved with a touch of his spur,
As Montana's wind began to stir.

Slowly they cantered down-the hill.
Moving together with practice and skill.
Once the cattle were safe and sound,
He knew he must ride into the town.

Something in the wind whispered her name
And he knew it couldn't be the same
Dylan had said Paint was back in town
Would she remember, he thought with a frown?

Paint's eyes watched the picture he made
Seeing him again made her so afraid.
Would he even remember her face?
She worked the bar, and she knew her place.

After all these years, she still felt this way,
She loved him from the very first day.
Wild as the wind and freely, he flew.
She stared at him now, wondering what to do.

Would they still share their dreams and fears?
How long had it been? How many years?
There was a sparkle in his whiskey-colored eyes.
His heart was as big as Montana's blue skies,

A typical cowboy; proud, silent, and strong.
Firm in his belief of right and of wrong.
Yet, to Paint, he was sensitive, gentle, and kind.
A rare breed of man, not easy to find.

All these feelings she'd buried deep in her heart
Afraid that her past would tear them apart.
Yet as he walked toward her on this day
All the years seemed to fade away.

When her Cowboy encircled her in his arms,
She surrendered, knowing no alarm,
He kissed her lips and thanked his saint,
At last, he had found his beloved, Paint.

THE LEGEND OF DIXIE DANDELION & JALAPENO JACK

"You no good, egg-suckin' dawg!"

These words were muttered under my breath out of fear of waking Buddy from his drunken stupor. Why? Because I was running from him. Where? Some place far and remote.

His jeans lay on top of the heap of dirty laundry, and I grabbed his wallet out of his pocket. Two thousand dollars! Business was good, but then again, drug dealing was profitable on the streets of New York City. I took half. My inner voice said, "Take it all," but I ignored the whisper—bad karma. I found my truck keys on the scarred dresser top, weaved through the trail of beer bottles, and slipped out the door.

The stench of rotting garbage and urine burned my nose as I dodged a mouse running down the hallway. I climbed into the cab of my Ford pickup and gasped at the dried blood stain on the front seat. Had the drug deal gone bad? The more I stared at it, the madder I got. I stomped back into our cracker box apartment and took the other thousand dollars. To hell with karma. My days of being a righteous Sunday school kid were over. This was Survival 101, and the first lesson was, to *get money!*

Returning to the truck, I popped open the glove compartment and found a roll of duct tape because, you know, no self-respecting Southern girl would be caught dead without it. My hands shook as I patched over the blood. The engine roared to life.

The gas gauge was empty. Damn him!

I filled the tank at Watson's One Stop, bought a Coke, and a map. In a daze, I stared at the red and blues lines that crisscrossed the United States like a spider web swinging from the porch light to the house. Hmm . . . I was born and raised in Georgia, lost my innocence in the East, and the Midwest wasn't far enough away. That left the West. I closed my eyes and prayed. My finger hit the paper with a dull tap, and Tucumcari, New Mexico, lay pinned under my painted fingernail when I forced my eyes open.

Buddy said I looked at life through rose-colored glasses. No more. I threw them in the glove compartment, vowing never to believe in happy-ever-afters again. They only happen in movies and fairy tales. A deep breath later, I headed West. Two dozen cokes, a case of Twinkles, and sixteen hours later, I crossed the New Mexico border.

The Roadrunner Cafe rested behind the post office in downtown Tucumcari. The mouth-watering scent of frying bacon and coffee drifted through its half-opened windows and pulled me from the truck with an invisible hand. The "Waitress Wanted" sign caught my attention, along with the stuffed jack-a-lope and coiled rattlesnake display.

"Howdy, hon. You come for the job or the joe?"

"Both." I laughed.

The tall, middle-aged woman poured a mug of coffee and slid it to my end of the lunch counter without spilling a drop. "You're hired."

"Just like that? No application? No references?"

"Don't need none. Can tell by looking at ya', you're the girl. When can you' start?"

"Now?"

"Sounds good. Lunch crowd be comin' in soon. New in town?"

I nodded and caught the apron she threw at

me.

"Need a place to stay?"

She didn't wait for my reply. With a toss of her bleached-blonde hair and a wave of her heavily-ringed hand, she motioned for me to follow her out the back door.

"This cabin belongs to my brother, but he's in the Army and won't be home for a spell. It ain't much, but it's furnished and cheap."

She unlocked the door. I jumped when an orange cat leaped off the roof and dashed through my legs. "That there's Sylvester. Crazy critter thinks he's a cougar. He and that paint horse out back come with the house. The flapper do-hickie in the toilet needs replacing, but other than that, everything works. Well, what'ya think?"

I loved it. True, it was small, but it had endless potential. The stone fireplace hooked me, but the back porch sealed the deal. My breath caught at the view. The Tucumcari Mountains rose from the ground like the lost continent of Atlantis, surrounded by trees and a variety pack of foliage. The gelding in the pasture whinnied a hello. "Can I ride the horse?"

"Till his legs fall off, for all I care."

"I'll take it."

"Good. Name's Peggy Adams. And yours?"

Buddy wouldn't dare have the law after me, but just in case, I gave her Mama's name.

"Mae Montgomery."

If I thought the morning was a whirlwind, the afternoon and late evening were hurricanes. The Roadrunner may be a hole-in-the-wall diner, but the place was packed. Everyone stared at me like I was an alien from Roswell. I chalked it up to being the new girl. However, when it continued at breakfast the next morning, I quizzed Peg about it.

"Why do they stare at me like that?"

"Well, hon, you can't blame 'em. It isn't every day they get served flapjacks from an honest-to-God living legend. Had to take a double look myself when you walked in."

"Me? A legend? Whose?"

"Dixie Dandelion. Honey, you're the spittin' image of her, what with your scarlet hair, turned-up nose, freckled face, and eyes the color of the Caribbean Ocean."

"Dixie? Funny name."

"Depends on your perspective. If'n you're from Atlanta, like she was, then it's perfect." She pulled up a chair and motioned for me to sit.

"Back in the early 1860s, the railroad built a construction camp here called Six Shooter Siding. It was filled with gunfights and gunslingers. Dixie cooked for the crew. Rumor had it she'd run away from an abusive lover. She was a feisty, petite redhead what didn't take any guff from the rowdy lot. Many tried to woo her, but she'd have none of it. Didn't want no man or the disappointments they brung." Peg blew into her coffee cup, took a sip, then continued. "But all that changed the day Jalapeno Jack rode into town on that snow-white stallion of his."

"Was he handsome?"

"Handsome? Honey, picture a Greek god wearing a black Stetson and a loaded 45 strapped to his hip. Tall. Broad shouldered. Dark, whiskey eyes. Square jaw. Sun-kissed face with a Tom Selleck mustache. Yuuumm, yum!"

"Why'd they call him Jalapeno Jack?"

Peg laughed and threw me a wink. "Dixie asked the same question."

"'Cause I'm hot and spicy, darlin'! he said, and swatted her on the butt."

"Oh my God. What'd she do?"

"Most thought he'd sealed his fate with that slap, but Dixie flashed him a smile bigger than Dallas. She fell head-over-heels in love with him at first sight, and he felt the same about her. She quit cookin' and rode by his side on that pinto pony of hers. They loved each other with a passion not even death could quell."

Oh, to be loved like that!

"What happened to them?"

"Well, that's the legend part. Jack got shot in the back one night and died in Dixie's arms. The story goes that she took him up into the mountains and buried him. No one really knows for sure because both she and his body disappeared. The Indians say their spirits roam the skies. The legend tells that on a full-mooned night when two stars fall from heaven at the same time, they'll walk this earth again."

She gave me an all-knowing smile. "Last week was a full moon, and two falling stars simultaneously streaked across the dark sky. Three days later, *you* walked into my diner."

"Oh, Peg you can't possibly think . . . It's just a coincidence!"

"Ain't no such things, sweet girl. Everybody's waiting for Jack to walk through the door. Personally, I hope he takes his time." Her chair scooted back from the table, and she gave me another wink. "You're good for business."

That night, I sat on my back porch swing and absently petted the wanna-be mountain lion's head. "It's just a tall tale. Isn't it?"

Sylvester only blinked.

The days stretched into a week, then into a month, and still no drop-dead-gorgeous, chili-pepper cowboy walked through the door, but that didn't discourage the patrons. They remain-ed true to their legend. Of course, it didn't help that I rode a paint horse, either.

The business was booming one late after-noon when the wind blew the door wide open, and a shadow filled the entrance. Everyone turned and gasped. I glanced up and instantly found myself captivated by a pair of Hershey Kisses eyes set in a tanned face with a neatly trimmed mustache shading full lips that begged to be kissed. He pushed his cowboy hat back off his head and strolled toward me.

"Howdy, little darlin'. How about some coffee? I'm new in town. My name's Jack."

I pulled on my rose-shaded glasses and flashed a wide smile.

"Hi. I'm Dixie."

A BOX OF ROCKS

My brother and I gave Mama a box of rocks for Christmas.

Mama always went out of her way to make Christmas special.

All year long, week after week, she squirreled away money in her Christmas club account and waited for that magic day in October when the check arrived in our mailbox at the end of the driveway. Then, it was off to J.C. Penney and Montgomery Wards to put items on layaway. Long before Walmart, layaway was the smartest way to shop. And with twins in the family, Mama perfected the art of stretching a buck.

That year, my twin brother and I wanted bicycles. Red for him. Blue for me. Sure hoped

Monkey Wards, as Grandpa called it, had them in the store. Night-after-night visions of shiny bikes instead of sugar plums danced in our heads.

The countdown till Christmas started before Thanksgiving. Mama bought red and green construction paper and a big bottle of Elmer's glue. After supper, she'd help my brother and me cut long strips and glue them into a paper chain long enough to stretch from one corner of the living room to the other.

"Mama, when can we get the Christmas tree?" became our mantra the first week in December.

"Not yet," she'd sigh. "If we get it too soon, the needles will turn brown and fall off, making a big mess on the carpet to sweep up."

No artificial tree for us. No aluminum one with a color wheel, either. Weary of our whining over the tree, she'd give in, and the annual Christmas tree hunt in the woods across the road began.

Dressed in bright-colored coats and stocking caps, we'd cross the highway, duck under the strands of barbed wire, and scout for the perfect evergreen. Jack Frost tagged along after us and nipped at our noses. The smell of pine and fallen leaves drifted through the trees like woodsy-scented potpourri.

Mama let us choose the tree and we always found the best one. She'd saw it down with

Daddy's work saw, and together we'd drag it back across the road and into our garage where the flocking would take place.

Tree flocking was an art form. We'd wet the tree down first so that the fake snow would stick to the branches. The snow came in a bag that was attached to the vacuum sweeper, then was sprayed on the tree. Messy and time-consuming but well worth the effort. When dry and decorated with glass ornaments—not plastic—that reflected the twinkling lights and silver icicles, our tree was a snow fantasy beauty to behold. Mama worked the vacuum until the year the bag broke and everything in the garage got flocked, including Mama. Then, my brother took over the job.

"He looks forward to it," Mama said in response to my pout. "You can help me make cookies and candy."

Mama made Christmas cookies and cakes to give to the shut-ins at church. I worked the monster mix-master with its large white glass bowl that went around and around. The speed controlled by a small metal lever on the side. Mesmerized, I watched the walnuts that we picked out of their shells weeks before swirling in the batter. I'd sit on the kitchen counter soaked in the aroma of baking cookies and cake and lick the sticky beaters clean.

But as good as the cookies were, Mama's fudge and divinity won top prize. Sugar, vanilla, and bitter-squared chocolate combined to make pieces of sweet delight that would melt in your mouth. Mama's kitchen during Christmas was a slice of confectionery heaven.

"Let's get Mama something for Christmas this year."

Surprised, I gawked at my brother. The thought of giving instead of receiving had never entered our heads before. Guess, at the ripe old age of ten, we were growing up. This new concept consumed us. Every day after school, we'd climb into the hayloft and ponder on what to give.

"Wonder what she wants?" I asked.

"It has to be special," my brother said, big brown eyes round as chocolate drops.

"How are we going to buy anything? I don't have any money. Do you?"

"No." He sounded defeated.

"We could ask Daddy for some money."

"No, it needs to be something we got for her ourselves."

"We could make her something."

"Hey, yeah. She'd like that better than us buying something. But what?"

"Let's look around the barn; maybe we can find something that will work."

We scampered down the ladder and searched the barn's nooks and crannies. Dust tickled our noses and dirt smudged our faces, but we couldn't find anything except old buckets of paint.

"Guess we could paint her a picture," my brother said.

An idea popped in my head. "Why don't we paint rocks instead? That would be different and special."

"Yeah, that's a great idea! But they have to be the right kind. Flat and smooth."

"Let's go to the creek. Bet we can find just what we need," I said.

Mama didn't like us going to the creek, which meant we went every chance we got. A thin trail weaved through the pasture to the little stream that gurgled its way around tree limbs and stones. The sound of bubbling water and bird twitters greeted us. Creek smells of damp moss and crawdads floated through the air. The stream was a happy place and one of our favorite hangout spots.

Serious and diligent, we walked the slippery creek bed, eyes peeled for the perfect stone. We decided that twelve would be the right amount. Six for him. Six for me.

It took all afternoon, but by supper time, we had a dozen of the smoothest rocks we could find. We hid them in the hayloft until we could work on them the next day. Excited over our project, we watched the *Lawrence Welk* show, Daddy's favorite, without griping that we were missing the *Rifleman* on a different channel. One TV with only three channels meant we had to share what we watched. Daddy suffered through *Mickey Mouse, Howdy Doody, and Popeye* without complaint, but the Lennon Sisters trumped everything.

"We need to wash them first," my brother said the next day. "The paint will stick better."

One by one, we hand-washed every rock with Lava Soap. Nothing, not even creek slime, and minnow grime, could withstand the pumice in Lava Soap.

"What are you going to paint on yours?" I asked.

Big brown eyes stared at me. "I don't know. What are you going to draw?"

Big blue eyes stared back. "I don't know."

"We only got red and green paint."

"I guess we'll color them like Christmas ornaments."

By the end of the week, we had a dozen painted rocks. Red with green stripes. Green with red stripes. Red dots on a green background. Green dots on a red background. Plain green. Plain red.

"We can use the shoebox my new Sunday school shoes came in to put them in," I told my brother.

"Okay. I'll sneak into the hall closet and get wrapping paper and a bow."

We wrapped each stone individually in toilet paper, carefully handling each one like a fragile egg instead of a piece of hard stone. My brother wrapped better than me, so I let him gift-wrap the box. He stood as lookout when I slipped the package underneath the tree.

The peace of Christmas morning shattered with squeals of delight when we discovered the bicycles parked under the snow-flocked tree. But as excited as we were over the bikes, we couldn't wait to see the look on Mama's face when she opened our gift.

"Oh, my. This is heavy," she said when Daddy placed the package in her lap. She read the tag, "To Mama. From your kids."

Agonizingly slow, she unwrapped the box and opened the lid. The look on her face was mixture of between wonderment, confusion, and amusement.

"They're rocks!" my brother said proudly.

"We painted them ourselves," I added.

No words.

Doubt wiped the grins off our faces. She didn't like them.

Such a stupid idea. We could hear her thinking, "My kids gave me a box of rocks for Christmas. Big deal."

"Thank you," was all she said with a funny catch in her voice.

Many years have passed since that rocky Christmas. My brother and I grew up, moved away from home only to return for Mama's funeral.

He and I had the unpleasant but necessary

job of cleaning out Mama's closet and
dressers. One dresser drawer pulled out heavy
and slow. I gasped when I recognized the old,
yellowed Christmas papered shoebox with the
worn tag attached.

"Hey," I shouted to my brother. "Look what
I found."

"Remember when we painted these?" I
asked.

"We thought Mama didn't like them," he
said staring at the faded colored stones.

"Looks like we were wrong."

Sitting cross-legged on Mama's bedroom
floor, I divided the red and green hard rock
treasures between us.

Six for him.

Six for me.

BUBBLE GUM MESSAGES

"Mama? Do you believe in angels?"

I shifted my gaze from the rain-slick road to my daughter's reflection in the rear-view mirror. The spark of newborn knowledge set her eyes ablaze with cobalt flames and tinted her cheeks a warm, rosy red. Ah, the wonder of youth. How I envied her. When was the last time enthusiasm caused my heart to race? Lost in thought, I missed her question. "Sorry, hon. What did you say?"

"Do you believe in them?"

An uneasy feeling crawled over my flesh. "What makes you ask?"

"I think Matt is an angel."

I jerked the steering wheel. His obituary

flashed before my eyes.

At age twelve, Matthew Flint died today of leukemia.

The sour taste of nausea hit the back of my throat, and I fought to choke it down. Katie unwittingly hit a nerve. She questioned my belief. My faith. Faith? What faith? God took my son from me. They buried my devotion alongside him. Cold words flew from my mouth.

"Katie. Stop it! Matthew isn't an angel. He isn't anything. He's just dead."

Oh, Lord. I regretted my insensitive outburst immediately. I glanced in the mirror and witnessed the heat of youthful eagerness turn to cold ash.

"Katie. I'm so sorry. I didn't mean that. I'm sure if anyone could become an angel, it would be Matthew."

"It's his birthday next week."

I hit the brakes so hard the seat beat grabbed my shoulder. "You remembered?"

"Yes. Even if I didn't, you wouldn't let me forget."

Jim heard the garage door close and met us in the kitchen when we came in. He handed a cup of coffee to me and smiled at Katie. "What miracles did you learn in Sunday school today?"

She tensed and lowered her gaze. "Later, Dad. I'm going to my room now."

He threw a puzzled look at me. "What's that all about?"

My stomach fluttered. I didn't want to discuss this. Jim and I argued over Matthew's death enough as it was. He called me morbid. I called him insensitive. "She thinks Matthew is an angel."

His eyebrows arched. It was an annoying habit of his, and it lit the tip on my short fuse. "You snapped at her, didn't you?"

Damn him. He knew me all too well, and I hurried to explain. "I didn't mean to. She caught me off guard. It's his birthday, and you know how I get . . ."

A hand shot before my face. Palm up. Like a stop sign. "Yeah, Linda. Trust me, I know. After three years of this, we all know."

His sarcasm irked me, and the urge to slap his hand away burned down my arm to my wrist. I yelled in defiance. "Don't you miss him?"

His transformation frightened me. Lines etched his square jaw, and empty eyes fixed themselves on the little swirly pattern that skipped through the kitchen floor tile.

"Hell yes, I miss him. Every twelve-year-old boy wears his face."

His voice faded to a whisper. "How dare you ask that. I can't even smell a piece of bubble gum without thinking of him. Lord, he loved chewing that stuff. I don't know how many times I told him to 'spit out that wad!'

Soulful eyes searched mine. "I would give anything to see him standing in front of me with a mouth full of that pink gum. But he's gone. I've released him. When will you?"

I fixed supper in a daze. Jim's question revolved in my head like an old 45 record. "When are you going to release him?" Good question.

We ate dinner in silence, so tense I looked forward to the solitude of washing the dishes. I heard the click of the remote, and the TV fell quiet. Katie would be curled in Jim's lap. It was their favorite time of day.

"Mom tells me you learned about angels today."

Her voice quivered. "Yeah. But I don't think we should talk about them. It makes her mad."

"She's not angry, just sad."

He lifted her chin with the tip of his finger and smiled deeply into her eyes. "I'd like to hear about them."

God bless that man. Excitement returned to my baby's voice, and without looking, I knew the "high-pro-glow" was back on her face.

"They have names like people. Some even have wings and fly. Don't you think it would be so cool to fly?"

Her words came out, tumbled and rolled like a snowball racing downhill.

"They watch over us. No matter where we

go or what we do, they guard our footsteps. That's their job. We're never alone. But they don't look like us. Not like people, I mean."

The dish almost fell from my hand. That was a good one. How would my level-headed, down-to-earth husband react to that piece of news?

"Well . . . Hmmm . . . They don't?"

Katie shook her curls and answered him in a confident voice. "Nope. Not always. Sometimes they're a flash of light or a wisp of wind. They leave signs for us all the time. You can't see them 'cause you're a grown-up." She paused and lifted her gaze to meet his. "Adults are confused about what to look for, too."

"Really?"

"Grown-ups want to see huge miracles. They're so busy looking for big signs that they miss the small messages. I mean, would you notice a feather in the wind?

"Daddy. I know Matt is an angel. I talk to him."

What conviction. My heart wanted to believe, but my head rebelled. The dishtowel tightened around my knuckles, and I stood spellbound, watching the scene before me.

Katie's small head rested against Jim's chest, rising and falling in time with his breath. He asked the question that burned in my soul.

"What do you talk about?"

She toyed with the buttons on his vest and

answered in a rather bored, nonchalant voice as if speaking with angels was an everyday experience. "Oh. Lots of things. I tell him we miss him, but he knows."

Her voice lightened. "He saw me get braces and laughed because I can't chew gum until they come off." The tone of her voice turned thoughtful. "I don't think angels are allowed gum. He knows how sad Mama is."

That straw broke the camel's back, and I dabbed my eyes with the dishtowel. Jim cleared his throat. "Maybe you should tell her that."

"No, she doesn't believe in God anymore."

"Well, why don't you ask Matt to talk to her?"

A pained expression crossed her face. It was the same look I gave him when he didn't understand something I thought was obvious. "It's not my problem. She has to ask."

Later that night, when we were in bed, I questioned him. "I overheard your conversation with Katie tonight. What do you think?"

"Either our daughter is the most imaginative child I have ever known, or she possesses wisdom far beyond her years."

"Do you really think she talks to Matthew?"

"Absolutely. Katie is still young and untouched by the cynicism adulthood places on life. She still believes in the fairy tale of happy-ever-afters and infinite possibilities. Yes. She talks with Matt. Maybe you should, too."

Katie's unwavering trust plagued my sleep with questions of spiritual importance. Do angels exist? Is there life after death? Can we communicate with loved ones who passed? At last, I surrendered to her advice and prayed for the first time in three years.

Please, Matthew. I need to know you're here. Please give me a sign.

Monday morning dawned all too soon, and I stumbled through the day desperately looking for The Sign. By bedtime, I felt betrayed by false hope and was convinced that Matthew would literately have to hit me over the head with his message if I were to get it.

Jim's exclamation interrupted my thoughts. "What is this?"

"What?"

He shoved his pants at me and pointed to the zipper. "This."

I examined the trousers. Some kind of a gooey, pink blob stuck to the fly. "Oh, good lord, Jim. It's just gum."

"How did gum get there?"

Irritated with his momentary brush with stupidity, I snapped. "I'm sure there is a logical explanation for it. You must have picked it up in the men's room at work."

Quite put out with my lack of intelligence as

well, he shot back.

"Well, I sure as hell wouldn't put it in my fly, now would I?"

The bewildered look on his face was priceless, and I exploded with laughter. I fell back onto the bed, smothered my guffaws with the pillow, and laughed so hard that I almost forgot Matthew's birthday was tomorrow— almost.

Matt's day broke bright and still. Clear blue skies covered the earth like satiny rich latex paint. I crawled from my safe haven of blankets and reached for my sweatpants. My hand brushed against something soft and sticky.

I tore into the kitchen, yelling like a mad woman.

"Jim. Come quick. Look!"

I held out the waistband of my pants. His mouth flew open.

Gum. Sweet, moist, fresh, pink gum stuck fast to the fleecy material. Alarmed at my outburst Katie flew into the room. I wheeled on her.

"Young lady! Have you been putting gum in our clothes?"

"What gum?"

The pure innocence of her question ignited my frustration, and I practically shoved the sweat into her face. "This gum!"

"Wow, That's a big wad."

I heard Jim's quick intake of breath. Mine stopped. "What did you say?"

"It's a big wad of bubble gum."

The reality of her statement hit the three of us square on the jaw. Goosebumps jumped like popcorn along my arms and raced up my neck. Jim's face drained of all color. Katie squealed with excitement.

"Mama. It's Matthew! You asked, didn't you?"

Something deep inside of me stirred and broke loose. Tears of relief held captive in my dungeon of denial and despair finally escaped and ran down my face. Katie was right, this was Matthew's sign. He didn't hit me over the head with it, but it stuck just the same. Elation filled my being, and I felt reborn. Life is everlasting, and loved ones are never lost. Matthew's bubble gum messages restored my faith and allowed my head to join my heart and believe in things not seen once again.

That evening we visited the cemetery. I stood in devoted silence out of respect for the orderly rows of headstones that marked memories of cherished ones no longer present. A lone caretaker diligently trimmed grass around their stone feet.

Kneeling at Matthew's grave and gently tracing the chiseled letters of his name, I waited for the usual rush of sorrow to flood my body. It didn't. Nor did the heat of repressed anger flush my cheeks. I took a deep breath, and the joy of peace filled my lungs for the first time in three years.

From out of nowhere, the wind glided past and caressed my face with its trailing fingertips. Behind me, the caretaker muttered and swore.

"Damn wind. Gum wrappers? Where on earth did they come from?"

A knowing touched my heart, and I smiled. "They didn't come from Earth. Let the breeze take them."

I ignored the old man's disgust and returned to the car where Jim and Katie waited. Together we watched the last light of day fade into the magic of twilight.

"The stars are out early tonight," he said, then winked at Katie. "Wonder which one is Matthew?" Right on cue, a star streaked across the sky.

"Show off." Katie giggled.

I followed the flying star's journey across the heavens and whispered a prayer of gratitude to its flaming tail. Thank you. Thank you for your messages of hope, faith, and love. Oh, and Matt . . . Happy Birthday!

That night we rode home in blissful silence.

FLOWER POWER

My life changed forever a year ago today:

The intrusive ring of the telephone at two-thirty in the morning shattered my life. I hate Alexander Graham Bell's invention because too many emotions dance along its micro-thin wires. Like its cousin, the telegram, a phone call in the early hours of the morning chills the blood, often signaling bad news.

"Morgan? It's Frank. Mama passed away. She went in her sleep, like she wanted."

The shock threw a thin shawl across my shoulders and clouded my senses. I struggled to understand my brother's words.

"Morgan? Listen. I can't think right now. I'll you back."

The line clicked, and the receiver turned to ice. I fought the urge to slam it against the wall—to kill the messenger. Instead, I crumpled to the kitchen floor, hugged my knees to my chest, and sobbed.

An overwhelming sense of loss washed over me, and I cursed God. How could He do this? Mama was my anchor. Who would I turn to for advice, inspiration, and most of all, love? How could I continue without her? I felt confused and alone.

Frank's words repeated themselves in my head like an old phonograph record stuck in a single groove. "She went in her sleep, like she wanted." Guilt tugged at my sleeve. I should be grateful God took her quickly, without pain or suffering. But why take her at all? Huh! My heart turned cold, and I renounced my religion vowing never again to pray to a God so insensitive.

The rude ring of the phone interrupted my bitterness. What a way to spend the night, curled on the floor, denouncing God. I answered the phone and forced myself to focus on Frank's voice.

"Morgan, when can you get here? I need help with the arrangements—you know—I can't do this alone."

"Frank, there are none to be made. Mama pre-arranged everything the way she wanted it. Don't you remember?"

"No. See why I need you?"

What he needed was a swift kick. Didn't know? Through closed eyes I traveled back and returned to a sunny spring morning. Mama sat at the kitchen table with her signature cup of coffee and forced Frank and me to listen. All funeral arrangements were made, bought, and paid for. My heart flipped-flopped at her dark words. How could she talk about dying on such a bright morning? I didn't want to listen. How dare Frank not remember.

Sometimes I hated my big brother's helplessness. How was I going to deal with Mama's death and his insecurity as well? I resented the fact that I would have to be the responsible one. Deep down inside, I was scared, and there was no one to turn to for comfort. I steeled my resolve and my voice.

"Okay, Frank. I'll be there this afternoon."

The lightness of his *goodbye* indicated that he had washed his hands of everything.

"Sis" to the rescue. I wondered, *who rescues Sis?*

I drove to the airport on auto-pilot. Thank goodness for sunglasses. Protected behind their shaded glass, no one could invade my world of hurt and emptiness or stare at my red-rimmed eyes and vacant expression.

Sinking into the softness of my coach seat, I watched Houston's skyline glaze over with pink, cotton candy clouds that floated easily alongside our wing tips. Soon, the candied puffs disappeared, and the Boston Mountains materialized below. The landing strip stretched before me like a paved *Welcome Home* ribbon. Chill bumps jumped along my arms, and my stomach fluttered. Coming home always affected me this way. I couldn't explain it, nor wanted too. The fact that I was home was all that mattered.

The pilot skillfully maneuvered the turbo-prop through the crosswinds and taxied to the terminal. The tiny cabin door opened, and I took my first deep breath of good ol' Arkansas air. There are many breezes that blow in the world, but none smell as fresh as the ones born in the Ozark Mountains. If they could be captured inside a bottle, the world would have its miracle cure.

When I stepped through the arrival gate, Frank broke into a relieved smile. His wheat-paste coloring and haggard expression made me realize that Mama's death affected others besides me. He held his hug a beat too long, and I felt ashamed for being so selfish and quick to judge his shortcomings. He was scared too. Now was not the time to be critical. We needed each other.

Frank weaved his car through traffic and spoke in an absent-sounding tone. "I didn't know she wanted to be cremated. Wonder why?"

The voice inside my head yelled at him. *Because she's a free spirit and needs to fly.*

I patiently replied. "I guess she didn't want to spend eternity inside a box."

He made a left turn onto Sixth Street. Pages of my childhood scrapbook turned in my mind. A shoe store stood where Grandma's house used to be. The old drive-in movie theater, where I spent many a warm summer night, transformed into a Supercenter. Pity. Frank interrupted my trip down memory lane.

"We're home. You just gonna' sit there, or come in?"

Teary-eyed, I shook my head. I didn't know how I would react to the fact that Mama would not be meeting me at the front door, and I didn't want Frank to witness my vulnerability. After all, wasn't I the strong, responsible sibling?

"You go in. I want to look around first."

I suppose to some people, a house is an inanimate object incapable of feelings or emotions. But this home was an exception. It was an extension of Mama's personality, and its rafters sagged with grief, and the windows blinked at me with mournful eyes. Sorrowful morning glories snaked thin veins through and around the cross-stitched nooks and crannies of their wooden trellis and watched me with rainbow-colored lids. The whiskey barrels on either side of the porch swing wept and spilled multi-colored pansy teardrops at my feet.

The porch swing. I traced its smooth wood with my fingertips and stepped back into a simpler time when the moon looked like a scoop of orange sherbet plopped into a starlit sky. The whippoorwill's lonely call echoed through the hills, and Mama would swing and listen to the symphony of the night. I curled beside her and searched the inky sky for falling stars to make childhood wishes on. At the time, I had no way of knowing how such an insufficient event as star-gazing would someday transform into a golden memory. Even though it was daylight, I glanced skyward in hopes one would streak past so that I could wish for her return.

Silly of me.

Frank broke my reverie. "Sis, if you don't mind, I'm going home. She died here, and it gives me the creeps."

Good. I didn't have to struggle to keep a stiff upper lip now that he was gone. My hand hesitated on the doorknob. What would I find behind the door? How would I react? Would I get the creeps, and if so, what would I do? I took a deep breath and crossed the threshold. My energy merged with Mama's, and instinctively I relaxed. Not once did I feel uncomfortable. How stupid of me to think otherwise. This was my home. There was nothing to fear.

Her delicate scent of lavender and lilac beckoned me to the bedroom. Half expecting to see her standing behind me, I glanced over my shoulder only to find empty space. The closet called to me, and not knowing why I opened the door.

Cotton blouses pressed trousers, coats, and shoes caused her form to materialize before me, and I felt the sting of fresh tears. A green scarf escaped its hook and sailed to my feet. I crushed the silky wrap to my heart and curled it around my neck in hopes it would give me a sense of comfort. That's when I saw it. The trunk.

Grandma's trunk, with my name written on it in Mama's handwriting, sat waiting for me. My heart leaped. Why was my name on the chest? It was obvious Mama wanted me to find it. Why? What was inside?

I shut the closet door and slumped to the floor. Oh, God, this was too much. I lifted my gaze to heaven and spoke angry words to a God I no longer trusted. What was I going to do without her? It wasn't fair. I would never forgive Him for taking her.

Even though I knew something important was waiting inside that tattered box, I couldn't open it. My nerves were as fragile as Mama's crystal tea glasses. The trunk would have to wait until another time.

Frank called later that evening and dropped

a bombshell on me.

"I guess we'll sell the house."

What!

"I swear, Frank, sometimes I wonder if you're adopted. I can't believe you would suggest such a thing. This is home. Our home. You learned to parallel park in its driveway. Remember when your motorcycle caught fire in the backyard? We decorated Christmas trees in its front room and ate Birthday cakes in its kitchen. How can you put a price tag on those memories?"

I felt his shrug over the phone.

"You're too sentimental, Sis. You live in Houston, and I have my own apartment. Besides, I couldn't live there anyway."

Sarcasm dripped from my tongue. "Yeah, I know. It gives you the creeps."

I took a steadying breath and spoke slowly. "Frank, this is more than a house, more than nails and boards. It's my sanctuary. I come here to recharge and laugh. Mama made it that way, and she knew true value is not measured in dollars and cents. Don't you understand?"

"Sounds like to me you have the decision to make. Move or stay?"

My breath caught. He was right, but my choice involved much more than where I would live. It was the tug-of-war between the heart and the head. Texas was career and money. Northwest Arkansas was happiness, love, and home. Which was more important?

I followed my heart.

Today, one year later, I returned to the closet.

I pulled the trunk to the middle of the bedroom floor, unbolted the latches, and opened the lid. Freed from their forced purgatory, gleeful ghosts of memories past took my hand and escorted me back into time. One by one, I removed the items Mama wisely preserved in the safety of that battered treasure chest. Old report cards, crayon pictures taken from their place of honor on the refrigerator door, my first doll, and family pictures gathered at my feet. All cried out for attention.

A faded wooden frame barked, and George grinned beneath its pressed glass. George was a spotted guardian angel with four paws and a stick tail. The day he died was my first experience with death. Mama planted Iris bulbs on his grave.

"Not for mourning," she explained. "But for rejoicing in his rebirth every spring when they bloom. Even though the bulbs lay dormant in the winter, they are reborn in the spring. Flowers are God's constant reminders that life is everlasting and eternal."

The tinkle of bells invited me back into the trunk, and I found Jim Cat's collar. Jim Cat read the paper with me and slept outside my bedroom door, protecting me from the things that go bump in the night. Mama and I placed him next to George. I planted the Iris bulbs.

Another picture caught my attention, and my heart stopped. A sorrel horse nuzzled me, and I traced his blazed face under his glass corral. King and I grew up together, and when he passed, my childhood went with him. Mama and I planted his bulbs together.

Tears gathered at the corners of my eyes as I wondered how often Mama looked at these pieces of my childhood. Even though she saved these mementos for me, I knew they were much more than keepsakes. Each picture, each memory, was linked in a chain that kept her heart connected to mine.

What twisted irony life bestows on mothers. They devote their lives to raising children to become independent, responsible adults, only to suffer great loss and loneliness when that mission is accomplished. Mothers are silent heroes. I would give anything to have told Mama that.

I began to place the pictures back into the trunk when a large envelope caught my attention. When I opened it, I realized this was Mama's last gift to me. With trembling hands, I unfolded the pages and read the words she wrote the night of her passing.

To my dearest daughter, Morgan,
It is night, and the moonbeams dance

on my windowsill. My thoughts turn to you. After Frank was born, the doctors predicted that I would never have more children. I refused to believe them. I prayed for you, and six years later, God answered that prayer. Nothing is impossible to God. Miracles can happen at any time. Never forget this. You were a blessing and my fountain of youth. Always laughing. Full of spirit and the love of life. You understand its magic. Never lose that. The day you left home, my side was one of my darkest. You knew. You brighten the shadows with small candles disguised as cards, letters, pictures, and phone calls. They eased the pain but did not cure it. I long to hear your voice outside my window, singing to the night creatures. So pure. So innocent. Crickets know many melodies, but not the ones that lull me to sleep, like yours. I fear there will be little time for porch-swing music living in such a busy city and working such hectic hours. Please, never stop singing. Now, my sweet, before I sleep, remember this. I will never leave you. I may be a butterfly, a wisp of wind kissing your cheek, a hawk playing tag with the clouds, or a flower waving gently in the wind. Whatever the shape, I will be nearby. Just look. Never

*forget the power of the sleeping flower
and its magic of rebirth.*

I closed the lid on the trunk and walked to the front room. Mama's urn sat on the fireplace mantle. (Another thing that gave Frank the heebie-jeebies.)

I walked to the backyard and didn't hesitate. In the magic of twilight, when stars flicker with soft lantern light, I released Mama to the four winds. Tiny specks of her spirit drifted over the meadow, past George, Jim Cat, and King.

I bought a guitar, sat in the glow of the sherbet moon, and sang to the falling stars. And I made peace with God. His forgiveness melted my resentment into the mist of the quiet night.

The porch swing swayed but not from the wind. I felt a loving presence, and I knew Mama was there.

Frank stopped by for coffee the next morning. He took his cup and walked to the back of the house. I heard glass shatter and his exclamation.

"Sis. Come quick. Look!"

I followed his shaking finger as he pointed to the backyard, and my eyes widened in amazement.

Flowers! Dozens of flowers carpeted the grass and stretched across the meadow. Pink, blue, yellow, purple, and Iris flowers painted with colors more brilliant than any known on Earth swayed gracefully in the summer breeze.

I took his hand in mine and smiled through tears of joy.

"It's okay, Frank. It's Mama."

He looked at me, then back at the flowers. Understanding lightened his features, and a small smile touched his lips.

"You were right, Sis. This house *is* more than wood and screws. It's her sanctuary too. No, wait. That's not quite right. It's more than that. It's her soul."

I smiled at his awakening, and my gaze returned to Mama's field of rebirth, sown with seeds of hope, love, and renewal. The house encircled me in its arms, and I caressed its frame with loving hands. This was Mama's house, whose soul I inherited—bequeathed by a woman, a mother, an angel. Her words followed my footsteps back into my home, and her voice whispered in my ear.

Never forget the magic. The miracles. The music. I will always be nearby.

Just look. Never forget.

A single tear slid down my cheek, and I vowed. "I won't, Mama. I promise."

Outside, the flowers waved their leafy arms in peaceful contentment. I lifted my hand and waved back.

Mama was home.

IT'S IN THE CARDS

On my way home for spring break, Mother Nature threw a temper tantrum. The rain pelted my car's windshield with fists of fury. Thank goodness I wasn't alone. My best friend, Tiffany, sat beside me and tried to look calm, but the paleness of her face betrayed her.

"Raven, can you see the road?"

"Not really. But this can't last forever. I just hope I don't rear-end someone before it stops."

A few minutes later, she yelled a warning. "There's a blue light up ahead. Do you see it?"

I slowed the car to a crawl and inched my way forward. The cars in front of me stopped, and I stepped on the brakes. A State Trooper sloshed towards us, and I rolled the window down as he approached. He tipped the brim of his *Smokey the Bear* hat in greeting, which caused a thin stream of rain rainwater to come through the window. I rolled it halfway up.

"Good afternoon, ladies," he yelled over the noise of the storm. "The road is washed out in front of you. You'll have to turn back."

I peered through the rain at him. "Is there someplace close by we can drive to?"

"Rivendell is about the closest thing to us."

I thanked him, rolled the window the rest of the way up, and looked at Tiffany.

"Isn't Rivendell where the Elves lived in *Lord of the Rings*?"

I laughed. "Yeah, I think so. Well, if it was good enough for Frodo, it's good enough for us."

"Hot damn." She giggled. "An adventure in the making."

I had no way of knowing how right she was.

By the time we found Rivendell, the storm had calmed, and a light rain fell. Tiffany pointed to a road sign reading, *Come to Celestial for a heavenly night's stay.* "Let's check it out."

The *Celestial* stood proud and regal. The desk clerk greeted us with a bright toothpaste smile. "Welcome to the *Celestial*. My name is Stewart. How may I help you?"

Tiff leaned into the large, polished desk and flashed a brilliant smile back at him as if to say, "My parents spent a small fortune on my dental work, too."

"Well, Stu, we need a room."

"All I have available are suites. They're $145. per night."

She reached into her bag and slapped a credit-card on the desk. "No prob, Stewy."

Stewart gobbled up the plastic. "It's the Theodora Suite, #410. If there's anything else I can do for you, just give me a ring-ring."

We rounded the corner to the fourth floor, and goose bumps raced up my arms. I stopped and looked down the pencil-thin hallway. Something wasn't quite right. I glanced at her.

She shuddered. "Kinda creepy, isn't it? It looks like the hallway in *The Shining*. With Jack Nicolson. Remember?"

"Yeah," I said with a nervous twitter in my voice. "Here's Johnny!"

I crossed the threshold into Theodora's Suite and stepped back into time. There were two rooms dressed in 1860's décor. A soothing peacock teal covered the walls of the first room. Golden stars floated on its background in a *Celestial* theme. A TV, microwave, and mini fridge graced the second room, along with a black velvet chaise lounge. I blinked at it twice.

"What's wrong? You look like you've seen a ghost."

I stumbled to the bedroom, all the while

keeping an eye on the chaise lounge and the woman who sat there.

"So? Who's on the chaise lounge?"

"What makes you think . . .?"

"Hey, it's me, remember? I know that look on your face."

"I just got an impression of a woman crying, that's all."

"Know what I think?"

I loved when Tiff let her guard down and allowed herself to open up. "Can't wait, shoot."

"I think this place is infested with ghosts, and they protect a deep, dark secret. The lady on the sofa is Theodora. This is her room."

"I think you are absolutely correct. And guess what? She's laughing at us." My mood sobered. "I don't think she's laughed in a long time."

"Maybe that's why we're here. To cheer her up."

"Yeah, maybe. But I think it's more than that."

"Let's go to town. I'm starved."

"Sounds like a plan to me."

"I'll just give ol' Stewy a ring ring. I'm sure he knows a good place to eat."

Our giggles started all over again as we walked down the staircase. I didn't have the nerve to tell her a man in a gray, Confederate uniform followed us out the door.

We ordered hamburgers at a quaint café called the Owl's Nest. The placemats gave an abbreviated history of the town. We read the tiny articles while we waited for our food.

"Holy crow! Listen to this." Tiffany's voice quivered with excitement. "The *Celestial* used to be a girl's finishing school back in the Civil War days. One of the teachers was a woman named Theodora, and she died a mysterious death."

The waitress brought our hamburgers and between bites she continued reading. "It goes on to say that the hotel is famous for the ghosts that haunt it." She glanced up from the paper and grinned. "I was right."

"Score one for Tiffany." I laughed.

"Do you have your Tarot cards with you?"

"Yeah, why?"

"Will you do a reading? Maybe we can find out who Theodora is."

Her request sent shivers racing up my arms. I was thrilled at the idea. "Let's get out of here. I need some candles and incense. Surely this town has a shop that sells that kind of stuff."

Ritual isn't necessary for a successful reading, but I love to set the mood.

I placed the candles that I purchased around the area while Tiffany walked behind and lit each one. The room sparkled with a soft glow, and the stars on the ceiling came alive and danced a tango with the flickering flame. Rain began again and sounded like tiny cat paws tapping on the window glass which added the perfect touch to the magical ambiance. I removed my Tarot cards from the silk cloth I kept them in and started to shuffle. The energy began to build.

Tiffany sat across from me, and I lifted my gaze to hers. In a soft, almost reverent voice I said, "Remember, the cards are for Theodora, and we need to look at them from her viewpoint. Don't hold back. Tell me anything you see, feel, taste, smell or hear. Nothing is stupid."

I threw the first card.

The Queen of Pentacles: "This is her."

The Knight of Swords fell from the deck. "A soldier. Brave. Handsome."

"That's her true love. Wonder what his name was?"

"David. Hmm . . . no, William." We said his name together and squealed with excitement.

She cleared her throat. "This is going to sound funny, but you said nothing was stupid, so here goes. You know that song called *Galveston?* For some strange reason it keeps running through my mind. What do you think that means?

"It's a clue, from Theodora. The words are, *She was twenty-one when I left Galveston.*"

"Oh my God! That makes perfect sense. Theodora and William fell in love on the beaches of Galveston during the Civil War. He was a soldier and went away to war when she was twenty-one."

A tear slid down my cheek. "He died in the war, but she never knew. God, she's making me feel this incredible love. I think William knew he was going to die. He's crossed over and has waited for over a hundred years for her, but she doesn't know and stays earthbound waiting for him."

Tiffany's sigh was deep and forlorn. "So romantic. Throw another card."

I returned to the deck and threw the *Page of Wands*. "They had a son. But I don't think William knew. I don't know what happened to the baby."

"One more, Rave, throw one more, ple-e-e-ease."

"*The Justice card*. She's looking for justice, or maybe closure for something, but I don't know why or what for."

The last card picked was, *The Sun*.

"Happiness. Joy. Rebirth. Everything is coming up roses." That's a great card to end this with. It means everything is going to work out."

"Wow, that was intense. Let's go to the lounge. I need a drink."

The rain stopped, and we sat on the balcony of the *Celestial's* lounge in a zombie-like daze. Tiffany ordered a rum and coke. I drank a shot of bourbon and chased it with spring water. Her eyebrows arched in surprise.

In the background a folk singer played her guitar and sang Patsy Cline's *Walking after Midnight.* Subconsciously, I hummed along while I tried to absorb the information the cards gave.

It was well after midnight when the bar closed, but I didn't feel tired. In fact, I felt recharged and restless. "Let's go to the stream."

I started back into the hotel to walk down the stairs when Tiffany grabbed my hand.

"No, not that way. Let's use the shortcut."

She took me to the edge of the hotel's wall, pulled back the vines and branches, and revealed a narrow trail of steps that stretched from the fourth floor to the ground below. The storm clouds parted, and the Man in the Moon shined his light on the path that led to the creek. I sat on the clay bank and dangled my feet in the cool water. Tiffany hummed Patsy's song.

"I didn't know you liked Country/Western music."

"I don't, but this song is stuck in my head."

Silence wrapped around me, the mist began to swirl, and I felt lightheaded.

"I miss him so."

The words came out of my mouth in a Southern drawl so thick I could taste the mint juleps.

"Mama and Papa don't like him. They say he's too wild and dangerous, and he'll break my heart. But I don't care, we're in love. Where is he, Jenny? Where is my sweet Will?"

She stared at me with eyes as big as dinner plates. All of this was too surreal, and my head swam.

"What the hell was that?"

My face burned, and I felt flustered. I searched for something that would ground me. In the background the hotel blinked at us with lonely box- framed eyes and drapery lashes. Her hand on my shoulder broke the spell and snapped me back into reality.

"Tiffany, doesn't it seem strange to you that we're out here at four in the morning and not one car has driven past, not even hotel Security? Do you see any spirits watching us from the windows of the hotel?"

"This whole thing is strange to me, and no. I don't see any ghosts looking at us."

"You want to know why?"

"I don't see dead people?"

I smiled. "It's because *we're* the ghosts."

"Rave, what's going on? Sometimes your hoo-doo, voo-doo talk is just too weird for me to follow."

"During the reading, Theodora's spirit came into me. Understand? I became Theodora, and on the balcony, you became Jenny, who I suspect is her younger sister. Think about it. How did you know about the hidden staircase? How did I know about this stream? I didn't question you about the stairs. We walked to this pool with only the light of the moon to guide us and didn't miss a step. You and I have never been here before, yet we know the grounds like the back of our hands because Theodora and Jenny did."

"The song! *Walking after Midnight.* It's another clue, isn't it? That's why I can't get it out of my head. We literally walked in the moonlight after midnight."

She laughed. "Ya' gotta' hand it to Theodora. She can come up with clever ways to get her message across."

"She isn't the only one. I didn't tell you this before, but I saw William, in the hallway. He was on the balcony, too. Why do you think I ordered Tennessee whiskey and spring water? I would never drink that, but a Southern gentleman would. They loved their bourbon and branch water."

"Yeah, I thought that was strange. But what are the clues about? What are they trying to tell us?"

"I think Theodora was pregnant with William's baby. In order to hide the pregnancy from her family, she accepted a teaching position at this school, and her little sister came with her. I think Jennifer—Jenny—and

Theodora would sneak out at night by way of the outside staircase, and go walking, after midnight when they were confident everyone was in bed and no one would see them. They came to this spring, and Theodora would tell her sister of the love she had for William and how worried she was he would never return for her. Now, do you understand? For a moment in time, we walked in their spirit."

"So you think I was Jennifer in that lifetime?"

"Exactly. But there's more."

"As if this isn't enough! Go on."

"At the Owl's Nest you read that Theodora died mysteriously, and I threw the Justice card during the reading. I think fate brought us here to find out how Theodora died and what happened to her son, but that's just minor compared to the main reason."

"I know I'm going to hate myself for asking, but what's the main reason?"

"Theodora and William were destined to be together, but their lives were cut short. Their passion has burned for years and must be expressed. Both of them are reaching out to us. We're their last hope. It's like a who-done-it novel that began over 150 years ago, and we have to write the last chapter. We have to free Theodora from this dimension and reunite her with William to fulfill their destiny."

"And just how are we going to do that?"

"The veil between the afterlife and this world is thin. Thin as onion skin. We have to find out what happened to Theodora, get closure, and then cross her over to the other side to William's waiting arms."

"Huh. Is that all? And I suppose you know how to do that?"

My laughter rang through the night, bounced off the trees, and rose to the moon above.

"I haven't got a clue."

Tiffany winked. "No prob, girlfriend. Maybe you can channel the ghost of Nancy Drew. We can solve the mystery. After all . . . it's in the cards."

THE JESUS CAT

YEE-OW-EE!
I shot up out of bed. What was that?
The alarm clock flashed 1:00 A.M..
Had I been dreaming?

MEOW. GROWL-L-L-L-L.

No, the noise was real. I turned on the porch light and searched the yard for the mountain lion that roared.

YOWL! GRRRRRR!

The sound came from the firewood stacked against the side of the house. I moved the cross-stitched logs. A pair of florescent green orbs caught the porch light's reflection and loomed eerie and large. I jumped back.

MEOW.

I laughed at my fear. The "mountain- lion-that- roared" was a kitten no larger than my two hands cupped together. His tiny bones looked like tooth-picks sticking out of his matted gray-black fur. I could count each one of his ribs.

I ran to the kitchen and opened a can of *Nine Lives*. When I put the bowl down on the steps, the little guy scurried out of his hidey-hole and proceeded to devour the moist food with grunts and tiny roars. He sounded like a jungle lion feeding after a fresh kill. I had a miniature *Mutual of Omaha's Wild Kingdom* taking place on my front porch.

He finished off the can of chicken, a bowl of milk, and a cup of water. Then, he returned to the safety of the woodpile and fell asleep. His little belly, swollen with food, lifted and fell with each breath.

"Hey," Daddy said the next day. "Did you know there's a kitten in the woodpile?"

"Yeah. He announced his arrival at one o'clock this morning."

"Well, he's waiting for breakfast."

I filled the cat bowl, amused as the little waif licked up every morsel, then looked at me as if to say, "Please, sir, I want some more."

"I bet if we opened the door, he'd come right in," Daddy said.

I laughed and dumped crunchies in the bowl. That's all we needed, another cat. Casper ruled the house, and I didn't know how he would react to a rival, no matter how small.

"He looks like Yoda." Daddy grinned. "His ears are twice the size of his body."

When I left for work, I knew when I got home, Yoda would be in the house. Daddy was a sucker for lost, abandoned animals, even though he would never admit it. The list of stray dogs and cats that visited our home throughout the years was as long as my arm. Some were dumped along the highway while others stopped over to rest and fill their stomachs before continuing on with their journeys to who knows where. None were turned away. Daddy said God sent them to us for a reason. It was our duty to feed and care for each one because they were God's children too.

Yoda moved in. He not only owned the house, but our hearts as well. Casper took one whiff of the little fur ball and promptly dismissed him. They grew to be inseparable buddies.

Yoda had the appetite of a horse. When he ate it reminded me of the scene in *Gone with the Wind* when Scarlett vowed she would never go hungry again. I toyed with the idea of calling him Rhett, but Yoda fit too well. Though he packed the food away, he was slow to grow into his ears. Other parts of his body, however, grew like weeds.

"You're either going to have to get that cat fixed or get him a loin cloth," Daddy said one day.

He was right, but I didn't have the money.

"Call Doc Hendrix," Daddy said. "He'll do it for less than thirty dollars."

A warning bell went off in my head. "Why so cheap?"

"He's just an old country vet. But he's good. He patched up ol' Shep's broken leg like new."

Shep was a collie that had been hit by a car and left for dead. Daddy rescued him. I never knew the dog had a hurt leg, and that was good enough testimony for me. I called and made an appointment for the next day.

Daddy went with me and held Yoda in his lap. The kitten purred contently and acted as though riding in a car was an everyday experience. I turned into a driveway that led up to a slumped, weary- looking two- story house. It hadn't been painted since the Civil War. Daddy walked with a cane and couldn't maneuver the rough driveway, so he waited in the car for me. Kennels of yapping dogs announced my arrival.

Doc Hendrix's office looked like pack-rat paradise. His receptionist was a marmalade she-cat that laid in the middle of his cluttered desk and blinked at me as if to say, "Whatcha' want?" His waiting room consisted of a duct-taped truck seat pulled out of an old Ford pick-up. (Probably the one lying dead in his front yard.) The tantalizing aroma of coffee drifted through the dust and stale smell of aged medical journals. It came from a beat-up, stained pot gurgling in the corner. A sign above it read, "Help Yourself," but there were no cups to be seen. What had I walked into?

Doc didn't look much better than his office. He was a big man with salt and pepper hair that stuck straight up all over his head like he'd stuck his finger into a light socket. He reminded me of a ruffled-up, cantankerous hoot-owl with black-rimmed glasses perched on his bulbous, red nose. I doubted the good doctor was a teetotaler. A cigarette hung out of his mouth, and ashes lay on the floor like a trail of breadcrumbs.

"Bring him back here, hon," Doc said.

Hon?

I carried Yoda to the exam room. It was spotless. Modern equipment gleamed in bright stainless steel and the pungent scent of disinfectant hung in the air. Doc Hendrix pulled on an immaculate lab coat so white I was tempted to put on my sunglasses. Maybe he did know what he was doing.

I placed Yoda on the table and turned to leave.

"This will go a lot faster if you help me, hon."

WHAT?

He injected Yoda in the back of the neck with a needle as thin as a mosquito's nose.

"All I need you to do is hold his legs apart."

Holy crap! What was this guy talking

about? "Me? Do you want *me* to help neuter *my* cat? I can't do that!"

My astonishment didn't detour him. "Oh, sure ya' can, hon. There's nothin' to it."

"I can't! Besides, his eyes are still open."

"Oh, trust me, hon. His eyes may be open, but he don't see a thing."

Yoda's eyes looked like melted, gooey, green Jell-O. I swear his eyelids were the only thing that prevented his pupils from sliding out of their sockets and down his face. But just the same, it didn't make me feel any better.

"Here. Put this on. We don't want blood to splatter on your clothes."

Doc Hendrix handed me a lab coat. Trembling, I sat my purse down on the floor and put on the jacket.

"Okay, hon. Grab his back legs and hold them apart for me."

I took a deep breath. I was really going to do this. No one would believe it. I pulled the furry, stick legs apart, turned my head to the wall, and squeezed my eyes shut.

The sound of crackling gristle echoed off the walls. My stomach pitched and yawed. Doc Hendrix grunted and cussed.

"Damn! He's sure got some tough little balls here."

Dear God!

"Okay, hon. All done. You can take him home now."

"You're not going to keep him overnight for observation?"

"Nope. Waste of money. Just take him home and put him in a dark room."

"A dark room?"

"Yep. When he starts to wake up, he needs to be in a quiet room. He'll remember the first thing he sees, so you need to have him somewhere peaceful. Because, trust me, hon. He's gonna' see Jesus."

I started to gather Yoda in my arms when Doc stopped me.

"Here. I got something better you can carry him in."

He handed me a grocery sack and placed Yoda gently into it.

"Now, remember. He'll see Jesus. A dark room is the best."

I laid the lab coat on the table and carried Yoda to the car. The yappy dogs jumped and grinned at me through their wire cages as if they knew what I had in my paper bag.

Daddy's grin was just as big.

I placed Yoda in the back seat and slid behind the wheel.

Daddy chuckled.

"You knew all along what was going to happen, didn't you?" I said.

"Sure. That's why he's so cheap."

Somewhere along the line Daddy had transformed from a strong, reasonable man into an old coot.

When I took Yoda from the back seat and carried him down the hall to my bedroom closet, the humor and absurdity of the situation hit me.

You know you're a redneck when you help neuter your own cat, put him inside a Piggy Wiggly grocery sack, and carry him to a dark room because he's about to have a religious experience.

I placed Yoda on a pillow in my closet and then went about fixing supper and washing the dishes. About an hour later, when Daddy and I were watching TV, I caught a movement out of the corner of my eye. Yoda weaved down the hallway like he'd been on a weekend binge. His spaghetti legs collapsed under his weight, and he rested for a few seconds before trying to walk again. It was pitiful. I got up and cuddled him in my arms.

"Poor little thing," I cooed. "Come on; I'll put you back in the closet."

Ten minutes later, here he came again.

"He wants to be with us," Daddy said. "Go get him."

Yoda spent the rest of the evening curled on my lap.

Did he see Jesus?

Yes.

How do I know?

Because Yoda was filled with the Christ

Spirit. He loved everyone. Unconditionally. When I was sick, Yoda curled around me and kneaded healing magic into my hurt with white, velvet feet. If depressed, he'd pull some kind of cute, kitten trick that would make me laugh. At night he'd lay on my chest and gently reach out with his paw and pat my face. I'd look into his emerald eyes and hear him purr, "I love you. Thank you for making me a part of this family, for feeding and loving me."

Oh, yes. Yoda and Jesus were the best of buds.

~ ~ ~ ~

Daddy, Doctor Hendrix, and Yoda have long passed from this existence into the next. I know they are in heaven because God especially loves veterinarians, old coots, and cats.

Some argue that animals don't go to heaven because they have no souls. Oh, really?

All pets live for only one reason, to love. They greet us at the door and brighten our day with soft purrs and wagging tails. They accept us for who we are regardless of our weight, color, age, or paycheck, asking nothing in return except an occasional belly rub or scratch behind the ears, a dry, warm place to sleep, and a full food dish. Can the same things be said about Mankind? Maybe it's Man that doesn't have a soul. If Man is allowed in heaven, so are animals.

I know, without a doubt, Yoda will greet me at the Gate. Because, after all, he does have a friend in Jesus.

ROSCOE AND JULIET

"Give all to love; obey thy heart"
Ralph Waldo Emerson

"Hey, Earl, where you going for supper tonight?"

"I don't rightly know, Sam," I said. "It's been too hot to cook, and pickings are slim."

"True, true," Sam answered with a nod of his bushy head. "Heard tell there's a new place down by the lake. Word is a widow woman lives there and always has something set aside for stray guests."

"Sounds good to me, but let's wait until dark. The traffic isn't as heavy then. Let's invite Roscoe along too. He doesn't get out much since losing Sally."

"Good idea. Darn shame about Sally."

"Yeah, she and Roscoe made the perfect couple." I sighed. "Poor woman's eyesight was bad, and she never saw the car that took her out."

Sam clicked his tongue. "It's a tragedy, I tell ya. But at least she went quickly. I guess that's something to be grateful for."

"I don't think I'd say that to Roscoe just yet if I were you. I'll meet you back here in about an hour."

Sam waddled off, and I couldn't help but chuckle. His stomach was as round as he was tall, and he looked like an egg with legs walking away. I scampered through the peach orchard and crossed the creek to Roscoe's neck of the woods and knocked on his door.

"Roscoe? You asleep?"

His deep growl greeted me, and he rubbed dark circles under his eyes. "Not anymore."

I ignored his grumpy response and invited him to supper.

He pawed at his belly and avoided my eyes. "Aw, I don't know, Earl. I think I'll pop the lid on a tin can around here."

"I ain't taking no for an answer. Besides, a nice widow woman runs the place, and ya just never know . . ."

His hazelnut eyes flashed. "A widow woman, you say? Well, I guess I could go, seeing how you're so insistent. Besides, a stroll before dinner would do me good."

I smiled. Roscoe was a crafty ol' critter, but he wasn't fooling me. I knew why he was going, and it didn't have anything to do with a walk in the moonlight.

The orange sherbet moon sat high in the inky sky and graciously lit the path before us. We padded along in single file and enjoyed the soft, springy feel of the grass beneath our feet. Before long, the muggy air of the afternoon yielded to the crisp coolness of the evening, and Roscoe sniffed the night.

"Smell that?" He asked. "Nothing's sweeter than a fresh breeze coming off the water."His ringed tail drooped. "Sal and I planned on moving to the lake, but we never got around to it. Now, it's too late."

"Don't talk like that, Roscoe," I barked. "Sam, shouldn't we be there by now?"

Sam gave the ground a good whiff. "Hmm . . . should be right around here. It's the third house on the left. Yep, there it is, but don't go to the front door. The food's around back. Let's go."

"Woooee. Look at that!" Roscoe exclaimed.

"Jackpot!" Sam said. "Just look at that big bowl of grub."

I wrinkled my nose. "What is it?"

"Who cares?" Sam said, and dashed by us to cram his cheeks full of the crunchy morsels.

"Here's the bag it came in." Roscoe adjusted his monocle and squinted. "I can't make out the name, Earl. What's it say?"

I looked at the checkerboard on the box and sounded out the name. "Purina. Hmm . . . must be French."

"You know what goes good with French food?" Sam asked. "Wine."

I laughed. "Raccoons and liquor don't mix, and we're better off without it."

Roscoe arched his back and hissed in a French accent. "*Au contraire, monsieur.* I could use a good merlot to cleanse the palate. My friend, John Bigfoot, tells me that the best wine around can be found hanging in trees in plastic containers disguised as bird feeders."

"Oh, what does that big, hairy ape know?" I scoffed.

Roscoe walked to the side of the house. "Ever wonder why hummingbirds zoom around so much? They're hyped up on joy juice, that's why. I'm going to look around front."

Sam shook his head at me. "Let's just humor the ol' guy. What can it hurt?"

A large crash and the click of the porch light answered his question. Roscoe tore around the house, clutching the stolen treasure in his paw like a dragon protecting a cache of gold.

"Busted!" He yelled and disappeared into the darkness.

A shadowy figure stopped at the corner of the house and yelled. "Come back here with my bird feeder, you thieving, masked varmint!"

Huffing and puffing, Sam and I scooted away to the safety of the neighbor's woodpile. The bird feeder lay empty on the ground, and Roscoe grinned at us with red lips.

"Whew!" Sam exclaimed. "That was close. She was mad."

"Naw," Roscoe said in a thick voice.

I looked at him in disbelief. "For Pete's sake, Roscoe, she called us varmints!"

"Yeah, but she was laughing when she said it."

"Come on, Sam," I said, exasperated. "Help me get this ol' fool home before we get a butt full of rock salt."

I didn't see Roscoe for a while after the "summer wine caper" and was surprised when he stopped by for a visit a few weeks later. He looked fat and sassy and had a twinkle in his eye. I only knew of one thing that could change a fellow that fast. I pointed my paw at him and grinned. "You got a girlfriend."

"That's why I stopped by, to tell you I'm moving." He flashed his teeth in a sheepish grin. "To the lake."

My mouth flew open, and I yelled in shock. "The Widow Woman?It will never work."

The hair on his back bristled. "Why not?"

"Well, for one thing, she's human!"

"A minor technicality only. Every new relationship requires adjustments."

"Have you lost your mind?"

A thoughtful look crossed his masked face. "That's just the point. After Sally passed, I felt lost and confused, and the loneliness drove me crazy. I thought I would never find anyone who would love me for who I am, until Juliet."

"Juliet?"

"That's the Widow Woman's name.

I stared at him. Bewildered.

"I felt guilty about taking her bird feeder, and I went back the next night to return it. She was on the porch so I dropped it and started to run, but her laugh stopped me. Her musical laughter sounded so much like Sally's that I decided to sit in the grass and watch her. She went into the house and came out with a big bowl of that delectable gourmet food and sat it on the edge of the porch. Of course, I couldn't resist temptation, and I climbed the steps and started to eat. I kept a wily eye on her, but she never moved. Every night since then we have dinner together. I eat and she talks. We have a lot in common."

This was unbelievable. "What could you possibly have in common with the human species?"

"She lost her mate too and is as lonely as I am."

I considered this. "Hmm . . . "I guess losing a spouse would leave a hole in your heart."

"Yep. All creatures—animal or human—crave love. It's a universal necessity. And the heart doesn't care if affection is animal, vegetable, or mineral."

"If I didn't know better, I would say you're sweet on that Widow."

"Juliet. Her name is Juliet, and I have to admit I've grown fond of her. She thinks I'm cute and calls me her Masked Bandit."

I stared at him in amusement. His large brown eyes turned dreamy, and he puffed out his chest. "It makes me sound romantic and mysterious."

"Yeah, you're a regular Romeo," I teased.

"Make fun if you want, but it's the first time in months that I feel appreciated and loved. She needs my attention too." He winked. "Maybe one of these nights I'll give the ol' gal a thrill and let her pet my head or scratch my ears."

I laughed. "Sounds like your mind is made up. Won't be the same around here without you."

"Yep. I'm gonna follow my heart and see where it leads me."

I watched him walk into the twilight of the evening and was intrigued when he stopped and waved to me.

"She's got a sister."

Oh, what the hell . . . I fluffed my tail and slicked my whiskers. Love is blind and ya just never know . . ..

SECOND CHANCES

I was born in a hippie commune and grew up to the sounds of *California Dreamin'* and *Flowers in Your Hair*. Hippies name their children after rather bizarre things, such as planets and mythological creatures. My best friend, for example, was dubbed Dandelion Moon, and her brother was Thor. I was named after a plant—ivy. Ivy Rose O'Farrell. Yes, I'm Irish and damn proud of it, according to Mama.

Dad was a rock musician with a stringy ponytail and a nose ring. He split before I was born, leaving Mama to experience the wonder of childbirth all alone. She worked hard as a waitress at a local café, slinging hash as she put it. Every night she'd meet me at the door with doggie-bags full of various delights, her ankles swollen, and her dreams broken.

Grandpop asked her to come home more than once, but she refused. If Grandma had been alive, she'd considered going, but Grandpop? That was a different story. Mama said he was a stubborn mule that wouldn't know love if it bit him on his rosy-red ass.

The topic of Grandpop wasn't forbidden; however, Mama never volunteered any information about him either. But there was that one Christmas Eve when she let her guard down. She didn't have to work that day, which was a rare treat, and we made the most of it. We decorated the tree, baked cookies, and hummed Christmas songs during the day. That night, wrapped in our cuddle duds, we plugged in the tree lights, ate popcorn, and watched *It's a Wonderful Life* on TV.

"That movie was your grandmother's favorite," Mama said with a catch in her voice.

This was too good to be true. Mama was actually talking about her childhood. I sat quiet and soaked up every tidbit of information she gave. Then, I ruined it— I asked why she didn't love Grandpop.

Her face puckered up and tears trickled down her cheeks. "You're too young to understand," she said. "Our relationship is complicated. It's just better we live apart."

"I think you should talk to him," I said. "Everyone deserves a second chance."

A sad smile crossed Mama's face, and she murmured something under her breath about the innocence of youth. She never did say she loved him.

Maybe that was the complicated part.

Personally, I think the problem was pride. Mama didn't want to admit that

Grandpop had been right about Dad. He predicted that the long-haired freak would leave her barefoot and pregnant. Of course, that was true, but Mama would rather die than admit it.

And that's exactly what she did.

I was twelve years old when I went to live with Grandpop.

The flight from California to Kentucky was one stop, which not only described the plane trip, but my heart as well. It took one beat when we took off and didn't start again until we touched down.

Mama flew in the cargo hold in a mahogany and brass casket. Grandpop sent money and arranged our trip but didn't come to San Francisco, nor did he meet me at the airport in Lexington. A gray-haired man holding a sign reading *Ivy Rose* stood at the arrival gate. I wanted someone to hold my hand and tell me everything would be all right, but I had to settle for a stranger holding a sign instead.

They loaded Mama into a sleek, black car, and when it drove out of sight, my insides cramped. How that was possible, I don't know. I felt hollow inside. Even though I didn't want to cry in front of a stranger, I couldn't stop the tears from streaming down my face. He reached inside his vest pocket and pulled out a handkerchief. His voice carried a thick Irish brogue that slid over his tongue as smooth as soft butter on warm toast.

"'Tis all right to cry, lassie. After all, you're only a wee one and ya' lost your mother. Ya' have a right."

"Thank you," I said and handed the wet handkerchief back.

His blue eyes crinkled at the corners, and he chuckled. "'Tis, alright. You may keep it. Ya' might have need of it later. By the way, I'm your Uncle Devin."

"Pleased to meet you. My name is Ivy."

"Aye, I know. Ivy Rose to be precise, after your grandmother." He looked to the sky and crossed himself. "May the saints preserve her."

"I'm named after Grandma?"

"Aye, and you're the spittin' image of her, with your copper hair and eyes the color of the Emerald Isle itself."

Why hadn't Mama told me?

He reached for my hand, and at that moment, Uncle Devin became my new best friend.

I climbed into his beat-up Ford truck that looked like a worn-out piece of junk with four balloons for tires, but it chugged along without missing a beat. I gawked at the scenery that flashed by the window. God painted everything in Kentucky bright green and made it smell like flowery fabric softener.

When we stopped to buy gas, he bought hamburgers and vanilla shakes. We ate them sitting on the tailgate of his truck. The sun warmed my back and melted the knots in my stomach.

When we got on our way again, I asked the question that had haunted me from coast to coast.

"Why didn't Grandpop come to get me?"

"Grandpop?" Laughter boiled out of Uncle Devin's belly. "Never heard him called that before. Tell me, did ya' think it unkind that he didn't come?"

"Yes. I was scared. Mama told me he didn't know love. I didn't believe it . . . until now."

Uncle Devin's hands gripped the steering wheel so tight his knuckles turned white.

Another mile passed. He turned and gave me his crinkly-eyed smile.

"Love can be a funny thing," he sighed. "Some people have a lot to give, but can never figure out a way to give it. Your Grandpop is one of those. When Katie . . ."

"Who?"

"Katie, your mother."

"Mama's name was Kathryn."

"Aye, so it was, but I called her Katie. When *Katie* ran off to California, she broke your Grandpop's heart. Your grandmother (he made the sign of the cross again) may the saints preserve her, passed when your mama was a teenager. Katie needed love and understanding, as did your Grandpop, but neither knew how to give it, especially to one another." He threw me a quick wink. "It's that damn Irish pride. It courses through our veins like hot lava and sometimes burns our brains so we can't think."

I giggled.

"Neither one of them would give into the other. Finally, they both gave up trying."

Worry put a hand on my shoulder. Would Grandpop push me away too?

"Ah, lass, Patrick O'Farrell isn't an insensitive man. The reason he didn't come to get you is that he's out of the country."

"Where?"

"Ireland."

"What's he doing there?"

"Buying the prettiest Irish mare ya' ever laid eyes on."

A horse! My heart leaped. I lived and breathed horses.

"Grandpop has a horse?"

"*A* horse? Lass, your Grandpop has stables full of horses. Didn't your mother tell ya'?"

Mama never said a word. Why? All I talked

about were horses. I read about them, collected figurines, and covered my walls with posters of them. I bugged her about riding lessons so much she'd cover her ears to block my nagging.

"It doesn't surprise me," Uncle Devin said.

None of this made sense to me.

"Now, child, I need to explain something to you. Shamrock Farms is a family business, and we all live there together. We have a family plot at Shamrock, and that is where your mother will be laid to rest."

"Shamrock?"

"Aye. 'Tis the name of our farm." He shook his head. "Don't tell me. Your mother never told ya' that, either. Shamrock Stables is home to the grandest racehorse since *Seabiscuit.* Have ya' ever heard of the great Triple Crown winner, Danny Boy?"

I gasped. Anybody who knew anything about horses was familiar with the dark-chestnut stallion Danny Boy. His blazed face and four white stockings had plastered every newspaper's headline when he shattered the records at The Kentucky Derby, The Preakness, and Belmont Stakes. But I had no idea Grandpop owned him.

"Shamrock hasn't produced a champion since Danny Boy. That's why Patrick went to Ireland. The mare he bought has the same bloodline, and we're counting on the foal she carries to return Shamrock to the glory days. That colt is our second chance."

"What if he is a she? Girls can run as fast as boys, you know."

"Aye, a filly would work too." His calloused hand patted my knee and he smiled. "Ya' got your grandmother's spirit, lass."

"May the saints preserve her," I quipped.

When I read *Gone with the Wind*, I dreamed of having my own plantation. Shamrock was that dream come true. It stretched before me like a patchwork quilt made of green grass, hemmed with white fences. I stepped from the truck and was greeted by the heady aroma of horses and fresh hay. A ring-tailed, calico-colored dog licked my hand.

"That's Mulligan." Uncle Devin laughed.

If Mama stood beside me, Shamrock would be perfect.

I spent the rest of the day meeting the aunts and uncles Mama never talked about. After supper Aunt Margaret showed me to my room—Mama's childhood bedroom.

The same blankets that wrapped her in their folds curled around me, and I fell asleep comforted by that thought, only to wake with tears on my pillow. The moon hung like a giant sugar cookie in the starlit sky and beckoned me to the widow with its cream-colored rays. I watched shadowed horses paw the ground and snort frosted mist.

Mulligan glanced my way when he heard me tap on the window pane.

I scurried downstairs and let him in.

"You can only stay until dawn," I whispered in his ear.

Neat freak Aunt Margaret would've fainted if she knew a dog was on my bed, but I was scared and alone. I needed someone to hug. I snuggled next to his silky fur that smelled like sweet, green grass and put my arm around his ruffled neck.

Mulligan became my second new friend.

The black car that had taken Mama away brought her home. They placed her beside Grandma. The coffin was covered with red carnations—her favorite. Everyone pulled a flower from her casket when they filed past. I reached for one but wasn't tall enough to snap it from its stem. A large shadow loomed behind me, and a bear paw hand broke a bud loose.

Grandpop.

The first thing I noticed about him was his eyes. Sky blue, but unlike Uncle Devin's, they didn't sparkle and dance. Framed by thick lashes, they were dull and void of all expression except one. Sorrow darkened their glow. My heart ached for him.

Grandpop needed to hug a dog.

I took his hand. Uncle Devin's eyebrow arched and Aunt Margaret gasped. I glanced up at Grandpop. A frown deepened the lines between his eyes, but he made no attempt to pull away.

Hand-in-hand we walked away from the past.

~ ~ ~ ~

Irish Mist *was* the prettiest mare I'd ever seen. I called her Misty. Grandpop tried to make her his first priority, but I refused to be ignored. I dogged his footsteps and made him talk to me, which was great entertainment for Uncle Devin.

He'd wink and chuckle, "You're a corker, Ivy Rose."

In an attempt to get me out of his hair, Grandpop presented me with my first horse, a lead pony called Buttercup. Butterball would've been a better name. The faded palomino had three gaits, a slow walk, a fast walk, and a reluctant trot. I glanced wistfully at the long-legged sorrel gelding, Firecracker, in the next pasture and dreamed of streaking across the meadow clinging to his back.

Uncle Devin followed my gaze and shook his head. "Ya have to learn to walk before ya'can run, lassie."

It was sound advice. But the urge to grab a hunk of mane, swing onto Firecracker's back, and race through the moonlight was a burning temptation that wouldn't be denied.

The night was bathed in full-moon brightness. Firecracker stood by the fence.

I climbed on the gate, gathered a handful of mane, and took a leap of faith. With a toss of his head and a flick of his tail, Firecracker wheeled and took flight. I bent low on his neck and melted into his shoulder. Copper curls blended with his flaxen mane until it was impossible to tell where my hair ended and his began.

The wind joined with my blood and roared in my ears. I shut my eyes and surrendered to

the power and speed pulsing through his heart and mine. Nothing could ruin my euphoria, except the look on Grandpop's face. He stood at the fence, waiting for my moonlit joyride to end.

Busted!

I slid from Firecracker's back and waited for my punishment. He handed me a bridle instead.

"Next time, use this."

A smile tugged the corners of his mouth.

"Your mother did the same thing on a night such as this so very long ago. I banned her from the stables for a month. She never rode again. Said I was smothering her, and she resented my need to control her every move."

He dropped to one knee and looked me square in the eye.

"She didn't understand. I did it for her protection. I'd just lost your grandmother. If Katie had fallen or been thrown . . . if she'd been hurt or killed, I would've never forgiven myself. I loved Katie. I couldn't lose her, too."

"You should've told her that."

"Aye." He glanced off into the distance. "I was too proud to say the words and ended up losing her, anyway. More than once, I've vowed if God would only grant me another chance, I'd

do it differently."

I touched his shoulder, and his gaze returned to me.

"He just did, Grandpop. And so did you."

Things at Shamrock Farms changed that night. Grandpop's eyes twinkle, and he laughs a lot. Mulligan is allowed in the house. But best of all, Firecracker replaced Buttercup.

On St. Patrick's Day, Misty gave birth to a blazed-faced chestnut colt with four chalk-white, knee-high stockings. We named him Second Chance. Uncle Devin and Grandpop broke out the Irish whiskey in celebration. They stood in the doorway of the barn and watched me saddle Firecracker.

Uncle Devin raised his glass to Grandpop in a toast. "Here's to second chances."

"Aye," said Grandpop. He looked at me and smiled.

"And may the saints preserve her."

THE FIRST BALLERINA

Once upon a time, there was an angel named Balla who liked to dance on God's cotton candy clouds. God loved all the angels, but Balla was one of his favorites because when she laughed, all the wind chimes in heaven rang.

One day God was busy adding sweet perfume to a new batch of roses, when He heard crying coming from behind the sugar-frosted rainbows. Salty tears would melt the rainbow, so He hurried to see what was the matter. He found Balla hiding under the bands of color. Her wet tears made the blue arc fade and stained her hands.

"My littlest angel, why are you so blue?"

Tears streamed down her cheeks, glistening

like diamond dust in the opal light of the clouds. "Oh, Father," she cried. "Everyone in heaven has a job except me. Ariel helps heal the sick, Gabriel rules the Moon, and Michael is a mighty warrior. Even the cherub twins, Twinkle and Sparkle, watch over the baby bunnies and kittens." Her lips drew into a pouty point. "Cherubim Snowflake says my wings are too small and, until they grow, I won't be allowed to do anything important."

"I think what Snowflake was trying to say was that your wings aren't strong enough yet. But you can still play. You like to do that, don't you?"

"Yes, Father. But I'm too little to skip clouds and too big to paint hummingbird wings. I can't do anything else."

"That isn't true," God said and stroked his white beard. "You can dance. I've seen you twirl and spin on clouds so tiny you must stand on your tiptoes to keep from falling off. Never think you're unworthy just because you're small, dear one. Everyone in my family has a purpose and is important."

He smiled, and sunshine covered the skies like a golden tablecloth. "I have an idea. Come with me."

Curious, Balla wiped her tears dry and struggled to keep pace with God's giant steps, but soon fell behind. With both hands, she grabbed his milk-white robes and rode on the hems until they reached the Pearly Gates where Saint Peter worked.

"Good afternoon, Peter," God said. "I'd like you to meet my new helper, Balla."

Delicate, silk wings dipped in greeting, and she smiled at the tall man with the silver halo around his head. But what did God say? His helper? What did that mean?

"Open the gates, Peter."

Peter stepped back, and with a wave of his hand, the mighty pearl gates swung wide. Balla looked through the clouds and gasped.

"Those are my children," God said.

"You mean the human beings?"

"Yes." God chuckled.

"What are they doing?"

"Anything they choose. I thought I'd given them everything they needed to be happy, but you reminded me of the one thing I forgot . . . dancing. They have the gift of music and can sing, but they don't know how to dance. I want you to teach them. It's a very important job. Do you think you can do it?"

Balla's heart beat so happily that sunbeams popped from her chest. "Oh, yes, Father, I'm sure I can."

The next morning a beautiful black-and-orange butterfly flew Balla to earth where she found two sisters playing in their backyard.

"I'm tired of dolls," the girl with the blonde ponytail said. "I wish I could fly. What fun that would be."

"I'll teach you."

The yellow ponytail flipped around, and the girl stared at Balla with large, green eyes. "Can not. People don't fly."

"Alice is right," freckled-faced Suzie said.

A small smile spread over Balla's face, and she sat in the tree swing hanging from the arm of the grandfather oak tree. "I can show you how to dance. That's how people fly."

Alice and Suzie ran to her, eyes wide with excitement. "Really? Please, please teach us."

Every morning Balla rode her tiger-lily butterfly to the sisters' backyard and taught them how to twirl, spin, and bounce with light, airy steps. Before long, other girls heard of the fun and joined the dance group.

Sally was very tall, and Balla taught her how to stand on one leg and stretch her other one behind her body. "Keep your knee straight," she said. At first, it was hard for Sally to keep her balance, but with practice, she soon learned.

Next, she taught them to pirouette and stand on pointed toes. "What kind of dancing are we doing?" Suzie asked. "It hurts my feet."

Balla didn't know what name to call her tiptoe dancing. It didn't matter to angels what things were called. These humans were strange. Everything had to be labeled, like cans of peas or corn.

"Well?" Alice demanded. "Tell us the name."

It felt like hundreds of eyes were staring at her, and she took a deep breath. "Ballet. I'm teaching you ballet and you're . . . uh . . . ballerinas. Tomorrow, I'll show you how to fly."

The girls screamed with excitement and ran home to dream of tippy-toe turns and wingless flight.

"Ladybug, Ladybug, fly me home."

A black-spotted ladybug landed next to Balla, and she climbed onto its back with a heavy heart. Tomorrow she must teach the new ballerinas to fly. But how? God knew everything. She would ask him.

"Ballerinas? Hmm . . . very clever." God smiled.

"I promised I would teach them to fly, but I don't know how." She dipped her head and long, sparkling lashes covered her eyes. "Can you help me?"

"You shouldn't make promises you can't keep."

"I know, but I wanted them to like me and think I was important."

A deep sigh came from God, and apple-dumpling clouds scurried across the skies. "I understand. Go to Saint Francis and you'll find your answer. But, Balla, never doubt that you're not liked. Remember, I always love you."

Saint Francis took care of all the animals in heaven, and Balla loved to visit him, but she doubted if he could help her. Still, God said he could, and God never lied.

Saint Francis walked by her side and listened to her story about teaching the human girls to dance. "God said you could tell me how to make them fly."

Francis laughed and sat down in the middle of a green meadow that smelled like strawberry jelly. Balla curled beside him and watched as one-by-one deer slipped from the forest into the pasture to nibble on the mint-candy grass. She laughed when the baby fawns leaped and jumped after the fireflies that zipped through the air.

"Tell me what you hear, Balla," Saint Francis said.

"Birds singing, bees humming, crickets chirping, the wind blowing. It sounds like music."

Francis smiled. "That's right. It's the lullaby Mother Nature sings every night. Now, tell me what the baby deer are doing."

"Prancing and tapping with tiny feet."

"Yes, they're dancing to the music of the night."

Balla giggled. "Their stick legs are so thin, yet they jump and leap into the air as high as birds."

"Kinda' like . . . flying?"

Joy spread through her and caused a pinkish glow to surround the meadow. That's it! She would teach the girls to leap into the air, move their arms in time with the music which

would give them the feeling of flight.

Mary Jane switched on the radio, and loud music filled the backyard. Remembering how the deer used their legs to jump, Balla taught the girls to leap with one leg and land with the other. Squeals of joy and excitement rang through the neighborhood. "Flying. I'm flying." Alice laughed.

Mary Jane could jump high and gracefully but landed like a rock. Peals of laughter came from the other girls when she hit the ground with a loud thud, and her pigtails bounced like rubber sticks. Balla felt her embarrassment at being laughed at. What could she do to teach Mary to land on soft feet? Again, Saint Francis came to her rescue. "Cats," he said. "Cats always land pillow-soft."

"Pretend you're a beautiful white Persian kitty with silky hair and velvet paws," she told Mary at the next lesson. Mary never hit the ground hard again.

Saint Peter, Francis, and God watched the girls dance every day. "Well, my Lord," Peter said. "Looks like you gave Balla an excellent job. She's a very good teacher. But, will her wings ever get stronger?"

God shook his head. "No, they will always be small and fragile as glass. But, if they had grown, little girls would've never learned the happiness and magic of dancing. That is why everything happens for a reason, and everyone has a purpose."

Tiny bubbles of laughter floated through heaven, and when they broke, all the wind chimes sang out.

"Sounds like Balla taught another girl to fly." Saint Frances laughed.

God smiled, and behold, it was very good.

WAX ON/WAX OFF

I prefer teenagers.

Male or female, it makes no difference. However, boys are my favorite; they're so easy to entice to surrender. I suppose this is due to their affinity for the physical—their insatiable hunger for the feel of velvety smoothness against their skin. That, and gloss. What can I say?

Girls like bling. Boys like shine.

Alejandro was such a boy.

Inquisitive, yet shy, stand-offish, vulnerable. He was ripe for the picking, an excellent addition to my collection. Hmm . . . now that I think back, he was my greatest conquest to date. No doubt because of the extra care I took in collecting him. After all, total absorption takes time and cannot be rushed.

In all fairness, I must confess in the beginning, Alejandro was not at fault. I can be very persuasive. Down-right sneaky when need be. But, as time wears on, innocence fades, and free will rises to the top.

~ ~ ~ ~

Let me interject a personal note here — in the end, free will is always the culprit. But, I digress. More about Alejandro.

~ ~ ~ ~

Poverty was Alejandro's facilitator. Not that he was to blame. The boy was born into an impossible situation. Deep in the bowels of Mexico, money was short. Employment was hard to come by unless one worked for the drug lords, which Alejandro's papa refused to do. Honorable of him, wasn't it? Hmm . . . well, let me just say, "you can't eat noble."

Yes, I know what you're thinking. I should've passed him by. Alas, compassion is not in my nature. Besides, I did him a favor. Gave him a way out of gloom and doom. Am I to blame for his love for polish and shine? No. As I mentioned before, free will is to blame.

He could've walked away. He chose to stay.

I started to nibble at him early by preying

upon one of his childhood fears and a particular, let's say, hobby.

Huddled deep into thin blankets, large brown eyes wet and shining with pent-up tears, Alejandro begged. *"Madre? Por favor?* The night is so black. Leave a light. Please."

"Alejandro, you are no longer a baby. There is nothing to fear in the dark, and electricity is precious."

"Por favor, Madre. Just a small candle?

Pathetic, isn't it? To be so fearful? Yet, in my business, it's a condition I look for. Fear makes my job so much easier. I believe some mothers share my affection for the emotion as well. Fear brings out a certain innocence, a vulnerability in children, a curious, endearing quality for some obsessive mothers. Anxiety keeps a child needful. Forever at her breast, so to speak. Perhaps it's a control issue. Whatever. In the end, Alejandro's mother caved. She always did.

"Si' hijo. Solamente uno. Only one."

A sly grin escaped Alejandro. Once again, his ruse had worked. Oh, sure, the dark scared him, but only a little. What he really wanted, what he really craved, was the candle itself. Peculiar, isn't it? It was the flame. It fascinated him. The way it flickered and danced. How it threw shadows against the bare wall. Some were so exaggerated, and a moth looked like a dragon. A little grasshopper morphed into a prehistoric monster with thick legs and long antennae.

But the flame was only the temptress.

His real true love was the melting wax. How soft, how pliable, how obedient the waxy edge twisted and curled under the slightest touch. Mesmerized by its suppleness, he was helpless to resist its pull even if it burned. The wound only stung for a brief time. Besides, the reward—a shiny, waxy blister—was well worth a moment's discomfort. The wax was kind. It never scarred. Never harmed him in any way. When cooled, the paraffin bubble simply yielded to his slight tug and dissolved, leaving a smooth, velvety patch of skin beneath.

As Alejandro grew, so did his obsession. No big surprise. I planned it that way. That's how I roll. My *modus operandi,* some might say. At any rate, when he turned six years old, an unexpected event happened.

"Los Estados Unidos? I'm going to live in the United States?"

"Si, hijo. With your aunt and uncle. In California."

I know what you're thinking. What a wonderful stroke of luck! Nonsense. Luck is so overrated. I orchestrated the whole deal. Why? Because California was a key component in the next step of my plan. Besides, I wanted the boy.

I always get what I want.

California was an exciting new world to Alejandro. The noise. The fast pace. The cars. Everyone owned a car in America. Fords. Cadillacs. Chevys.

"*Ay Caramba, Tio'*. Uncle, those Corvette Stingrays! So sleek. So fast and shiny."

California also brought elementary school and a brand-new twist to the boy's fascination for wax . . . the scent of Crayola Crayons.

"So many colors, *Tia'*."

"Yes. Many to choose from. Nothing smells as wonderful as a new box of crayons. *Verdad*? True?"

Alejandro couldn't agree with his aunt more. The sticky, sweet smell that hit him square in the face when he opened the 24-pack of colors made him giddy. He itched to use them. But not for coloring. For burning. For melting. However, he soon discovered —the hard way I might add —the unforgiving nature of the colorful, waxy sticks. Their bite was not as gentle as their beeswax cousin's. They burned hotter and stung longer. He best take care.

But, as we all know, accidents happen.

As is the case with most addicts, and make no mistake about it, by now, Alejandro was hooked; he soon grew bored with only watching the flame and wax and decided to experiment. To up his game, he dipped the tip of his #2 pencil into the melting ooze again and again. How many layers could he add before the whole ball of wax (so to speak) broke off? The trick amused him. It aggravated the hell out of his best friend, Billy Masters.

"Dude. You're so wack; what's the deal with wax, anyway? You're obsessed."

Billy didn't understand. No one did, for that matter.

Late one night, it happened. The pencil slipped, the bowl overturned, and hot wax coated his hand.

"Jesus, Mary, and Joseph!"

Oops. Sorry. I forgot to mention Alejandro cussed like a sailor. Said it made him feel more like a real American teenager.

"What'cha do to your hand, Dude?" Billy Masters asked the next day. "You got it wrapped like you're some kind of mummy or something."

"Burned it."

"Aw, Dude. Not the wax thing again."

"Naw. Steam from a broken hose on a carpet cleaner."

Another note: junkies lie.

"Better go see a doctor. Don't want to get it infected."

"It's okay. I put ointment on it. No big deal."

Lie number two.

~ ~ ~ ~

Let me interrupt for a second. Earlier I mentioned how compassion was not in my wheelhouse. I'm not completely heartless, however. I throw little hints now and again. Small warnings. The scorched hand was a sign. Play with fire, ya gonna' get burned. (so apropos, don't you think?) As I said, he could've walked away. He *should've* walked away.

Again, not my fault.

~ ~ ~ ~

The blistered hand did heal, but the new skin came in wrinkled, not at all baby-butt smooth. (This, too, was a hint. I really did try my best to warn him.) To make matters worse, one finger still remained encased in paraffin. No gentle tug peeled the wax away. Hard scrubbing with hot water and soap failed as well. While this puzzled Alejandro a great deal, he wasn't overly concerned. *Give it time. It'll wear off. Besides, it's only my pinkie finger. It looks awesome!*

The takeover had begun.

I used Billy Masters to seal the deal.

Not the brightest of students and not at all interested in isosceles triangles or theories, Billy cheated on his geometry final by copying off his best friend's paper. Alejandro was a whiz at math and had no problem sharing his answers with the coolest kid in school. Even at that, Billy passed by the skin of his teeth with only a D. Still, he passed. That's all that mattered.

"Dude. I've been thinking." Billy said one lazy California afternoon. Bored and restless, he and Alejandro walked the sandy beach and ogled the girls tanning by the turquoise water.

"You? Thinking?" Alejandro teased. "About what?"

"How I can repay you for letting me cheat off you all semester."

"Not necessary. No big deal."

"It is to me. My old man would've clobbered me good if I'd failed."

"Okay. You think of anything?"

"Yep, sure did. I got us summer jobs detailing cars."

"Qui'? What? Washing and vacuuming all day? Thanks, but no thanks."

"Dude. Hear me out. It's good money. But the best part? You can *wax* all the little red Corvettes your heart desires."

"Wax?"

"I knew you'd love that. Dude, I don't understand your obsession with wax. Pot? Meth? I get. But wax? It's creepy. Unnatural. But I owe ya one, and to each his own. I figured car wax would be your ultimate high."

He laughed. "One thing's for sure; you won't ever play with those freaking crayons ever again."

No truer words were ever spoken.

His first day on the job, Alejandro walked into Valley View Chevrolet and wondered if the dealership was heaven in disguise. Chrome and shine everywhere! The floors, buffed to a high sheen, looked like an endless glass mirror beneath his Nike Airs.

Simoniz Car Shine was a gift from the gods.

The wax went on so effortlessly and smoothly. Like sharp blades across frosted ice, the paste glided across the car's fenders and hood. The opposite was just as true. The wax came off in one beautiful, fluent swipe leaving a shine so brilliant Alejandro could see his own reflection smiling back at him. The wax on/wax off process fascinated him. The smell and feel of the polish consumed him. Working well past quitting time, Alejandro couldn't get enough of the polish.

"Dude. Let's go home."

"Uno minuto. One more minute."

One minute stretched into thirty, then sixty.

"You're sick, Dude. I'm outta here." Billy gave up and went home.

Alejandro didn't care. He was alone now and free to indulge in his secret desire. The latex gloves he was instructed to wear to protect his hands immediately flew into the trash. Dipping his fingers into the supple, cool paste, he rubbed his hands together in sheer ecstasy. Never mind the slight tingle and burn as his skin absorbed the wax.

He couldn't explain the overpowering need for the wax nor did he care to. Never had he felt more energized, more alive. Exhilarated, he moved on to other brands. Turtle Wax. Mothers. Chemical Guys. Flushed with euphoria, he failed to notice the waxy film crawling up his arms, chest, and legs.

~ ~ ~ ~

Let me pause for a moment. It's vital that you understand what is happening here. Just like a heroin addict, Alejandro could no longer live without his fix. The harmless playing around with dripping candles had turned into something far more involved, more dangerous. No longer content with the feel, smell, and rush of wax, Alejandro yearned to become one with the polish.

~ ~ ~ ~

Orange Carnauba was his swan song.

The soft citrus-scented wax smelled delicious and reminded Alejandro of his favorite soda—Orange Crush. This was the last straw. More than anything, he wished for a way to let the wax totally devour him. He wanted to swim in it. Drown in its scent.

Oblivious to the fact that his body was fast changing from flesh into a thin waxy film, he racked his brain for the pinnacle of rushes. Frantic, he took another deep whiff of the Orange Carnauba. Oh, my God! That's it! He would eat it!

Common sense made a last-ditch effort to reach him. He hesitated. Eat it? What was he thinking? Wax was poison, wasn't it? Like a lazy lover, the scent of Orange Carnauba reached for him. *Only a little bite. That's all.* Surely it wouldn't be enough to kill him.

He ate a little dab. Nothing. Just one more bite. No big deal. Right?

Wrong.

Warm blood congealed.

Clogged with goo, thin veins collapsed.

Lungs hammered for one deep breath, only to fail.

At the last minute, Alejandro realized his sweet, kind wax had turned on him. No longer a gentle comfort but a cold-blooded murderess.

He tried to scream for help, but his tongue, a thick glob of wax by now, wouldn't work.

He choked as a pasty film coated his throat.

A beating heart sputtered. Then died.

A mind is a terrible thing to waste. Human life is even worse.

Covered in wax from head to toe, internal organs completely smothered in thick, gelatinous sludge, Alejandro had gotten his last wish. No longer flesh and blood, he was now a block of the very wax he so passionately loved and desperately needed.

~ ~ ~ ~

Just an observation of mine: God turned Lot's wife into a pillar of salt. I turned Alejandro into a block of wax. Not that I equate myself with the All-Mighty. There is no need to. People do that for me.

~ ~ ~ ~

Oh. You may be wondering about Billy Masters.

After a few days, Billy stopped looking for Alejandro. He quit his job at the dealership, however, opting for a better one in Hollywood working at Madame Tussaud's. There was just something fascinating about all those wax statues. Ironic, isn't it?

For some unknown reason, he was especially drawn to the wax figure of a dark-haired Mexican boy with big, brown eyes.

Dude looks so real. Like an actual live person.

Well, Billy. That's because he was . . . once. You cheated off his paper. Remember?

~ ~ ~ ~

I leave you with one last thought: Perhaps you think me twisted. Socially unacceptable. An evil sickness. I beg to differ. I am neither good nor bad.

I am simply a choice.

I am Addiction.

THE WITCH OF MOON HOLLOW

I never would've gone witch hunting that Halloween had it not been for Loony Lonnie.

"There's a witch what lives in Moon Hollow."

"Oh, bull!"

This came from my best friend, Butch who always spoke his mind. A trait I greatly admired.

"You're making that up just 'cause it's Halloween. I've been through Moon Hollow plenty of times. Never seen a witch."

Loony Lonnie shrugged his ape-like shoulders and shook his head causing his carrot- orange hair to flop into his eyes. "She only shows herself on Halloween. Rest of the time, you don't notice her. But on Halloween night, she comes out. To cast spells and *fly*."

"On a broom stick?"

"You're such a moron." Lonnie scoffed and punched me in the arm. An irrigating habit, not to mention, painful. I didn't have the nerve to stop him. "How else do witches fly?"

Oh, how I wanted to smack that goofy look off his face. Mom made me promise never to fight. I liked to tell myself that's why I never punched him but the truth was I couldn't. My arms were spaghetti thin and about as strong as soup. Lonnie would've cleaned my clock.

I raced up the porch steps, grateful to be home. Mom wasn't there. Working late. Since it wasn't a school night, I could stay up and watch all the TV I wanted. I fell asleep on the couch. The sound of Mom's key turning in the door made me jump.

"Hi, sweetheart," she said and kissed my forehead.

Mom worked two jobs and never complained. I hated it, but didn't dare tell her so. No matter how late, she always took the time to tuck me into bed at night and kiss the top of my head.

Dad passed away seven years ago, but she missed him like it was yesterday. Her friends tried to fix-her-up with their single men friends but after a few dates she always dumped them. "A good man is hard to find," was her favorite excuse.

I prayed every night she found someone.

I didn't have the nerve to tell her that, either.

"I work a double-shift tomorrow."

She tucked the covers around me extra tight that night and kissed my head twice. "Thanks for understanding. You're a good man." She winked. "They're hard to find, you know."

I basked in the glow of being called her man even though I was just a puny kid.

Saturday morning dawned as the perfect Halloween day. Not too cold, not too hot. Mom left for work long before I crawled out of bed. She didn't worry about leaving me alone because I was responsible. Chicken was more like it. Between mouthfuls of *Captain Crunch* cereal, I phoned Butch only to find out he was at his grandmother's for the weekend. Bummer. All day and half the night to myself. What to do?

I finished most of my chores. While putting the folded laundry in Mom's bedroom, I noticed the picture of Dad that sat on the nightstand. A lump the size of a marble grew in my throat. Sure did miss him. That's when the idea popped into my head.

I'd get the witch to make a love spell for Mom!

A variety pack of huge trees stood guard over Moon Hollow like giant knights in leafy armor. It was a wooded wonderland in the daylight, but spooky as all-get-out at night.

Leaves and pine needles littered the ground like broken bags of potato chips and my footsteps sounded like *Rice Crispy* cereal . . . snap, crackle, and pop. My insides tingled when the cedar-and-pine dipped air hit my lungs.

Something shiny caught my attention. My heart fluttered.

A black Ford Mustang convertible sat not more than five feet away from me. Sleek, smooth, powerful. Speed rippled beneath my hand when I touched its doors and fenders. Totally awesome would-be Butch's word for it. Anything cool was always totally awesome to Butch.

"Like it?"

I whirled and gasped at the woman standing behind me. Where had she come from?

"Yeah. Bet it's fast."

"Oh, it can fly." Her voice purred. "You must be thirsty walking all this way. Come on in, I'll find you something to drink."

I nodded and followed her bouncing jet-black ponytail into the house that smelled like apple pie and reminded me of Snow White's cottage.

A house and car in the middle of the woods

should've been strange to me, but I didn't question it. For some reason, all normal thought vanished the minute I stepped into the hollow.

Her face broke into a smile when she handed me a glass of ice-cold milk and our hands touched. Heat raced up my neck. Green eyes, outlined in black, glowed so bright that it was hard not to fall into them. She smelled like honeysuckle. Kinda' mysterious looking and very pretty.

I was ten years old and in love.

"My name is Morrigan. What's yours?"

"Jimmie." Such a kid's name. I cleared my throat, and in my best James Bond voice, I tried again. "Bryant. James Logan Bryant."

She was impressed. I could tell by the way she grinned.

"That's a good, strong name. Now, James Logan, what are you doing in Moon Hollow?"

"Looking for the witch."

I was such a moron. Of all of the things I could've said, that was the stupidest. I expected her to laugh in my face. Instead, she arched her right eyebrow. Only the right. The left stayed in place. Totally awesome.

I hurried to explain. "Loony Lonnie said a witch lives in the Hollow, and it's important that I find her."

Again, the eyebrow rose.

"He's not really loony; we just call him that.

He told our first-grade teacher he couldn't learn to read because his mother accidentally dropped him on his head when he was a baby, and it made him loony."

I was rambling.

This time she did laugh. Low and musical like the wind chimes that hung on her front porch.

"Hmm . . . I see. Why do you need to talk to the witch?"

This was going to sound so dumb. "I need a love spell."

Both eyebrows jumped.

"Oh, not for me," I hastily explained. "For Mom. She's lonely. She won't say so, but I know it's true 'cause sometimes I hear her crying. She deserves someone to care and love her."

"And what about you? Aren't you just as worthy?"

I'd never thought about that. "Well, sure, but Mom needs someone more."

She pulled my eyes into hers. Sounds funny, but I felt the tug.

"That's very noble of you, James Logan. To put someone else's feelings before yours is not only gallant but the highest love there is. What does this witch look like?"

"Oh, you know. Green skin, pointy hat, big warts, ugly."

A faint smile pulled at her lips. "I haven't

seen anyone like that in the Hollow, sorry. But, I think I can help with a love spell."

She got up and went into another room, then came back with a heart-shaped box, the kind Valentine candy comes in, a pot of black ink, some funny-looking paper, a quill pen, a jar full of something red, and a pink-colored stone.

"What kind of man does your mama like?"

"Don't really know." I shrugged my shoulders. "A good one is all she ever says."

"Take the pen, dip it in the ink and write that on the paper along with any other ideas you have about the kind of man your mama would want."

"Strange looking paper."

"It's called parchment. Always write your spell on parchment with black ink."

Totally awesome.

"When you're finished, put the rose-quartz and paper in the box," she said and unscrewed the jar lid. The sweet scent of flowers filled the room. "These are rose petals, for passion. Sprinkle them in the box around the paper. Seal the edges with the candle wax. Now, take your spell box home and burn it."

What? After all this work? "Burn it?"

"Yes. All your wishes are captured inside the box. Burning it will release their intent into smoke that will carry out into the universe and bring the man you're looking for."

"Gosh, how long will that take?"

"When you no longer seek him, he will come."

I didn't understand, but it was getting late and I didn't have time for her to explain. Had to run. Sure didn't want to get caught in the woods at night.

"Thank you for helping me, but I gotta' hurry home."

Morrigan walked outside and took my hand in hers. Fingertips painted scarlet red sent chills racing up my arm. She bent down and stared straight into my eyes. Mint green melted into chocolate brown. Even if I wanted to, I couldn't have looked away.

"There is nothing to fear in these woods. Daylight will not fade until you reach home."

How she knew that, I don't know, but the sun waited to go down until I hit my front steps.

I put the spell box in the barbeque grill and set it on fire. Pink and red oozed into blue smoke that circled the back porch and faded into the night. Then, it hit me.

Morrigan was the witch of Moon Hollow!

Even if it was dark as pitch, I had to tell her how sorry I was for saying witches had green skin and warts. The flashlight's beam lit the way and I raced down the wooded trail. My heart pounded, my side ached, but I didn't stop. Lose my nerve if I did. Pain stabbed hard and forced me to slow down and walk to the edge of the woods.

A hooded figure stood tall in the middle of the clearing, her arms raised high to the star-infested sky.

The flashlight crashed to the ground. Eyes wide. Mouth open. I stood frozen to the spot.

Wind, crisp as a bite from a red, juicy apple, nipped my face and bent tree tops to the ground, only to snap them back into place. Thunder cracked. The moon bobbed between the clouds like a silver cork in an inky ocean. Yellow lightning zigzagged to the ground and caught the figure's face in its flash.

Morrigan.

Coal-black hair, loose and long, whipped about her face. A screech owl screamed. A wolf howled. The hairs on my arm stood straight up. Lightning tore the sky again. Her voice, clear and strong, cut through the night and rang like a crystal bell through the frosty air.

"I, Morrigan, Warrior Goddess, do hereby command and summon thee:
From the Sun, I take strength and stamina.
From the Moon, I take beauty and grace.
From the wind, I take power and speed."

She clapped her hands together three times. For a heartbeat everything stood still.

Something came up behind me. Goose

bumps crawled up my back like thousands of red ants. No way was I going to turn and look.

A horse glided past on giant wings black as the night in which he was conjured. With arched neck and tail he pranced to Morrigan's side. Her cheek to his, she hugged the black's shoulders like he was a friend returned from a long time away. She vaulted onto his back.

Casting a glance over her shoulder, she found me. A smile, half-pleased, half-mysterious looking, touched blood-red lips, and she motioned me to her side. Without a word, she lifted me onto the mustang's back, placing me in front of her. Warm breath on the back of my neck made me shiver and I heard her low laugh.

"Rith!"

With a toss of his head, the horse broke into a run. Faster. Faster. Wind whipped tears into my eyes. Trees and grass blurred. When I thought it impossible for the stallion to gallop any faster, his wings unfurled and lifted us into the air.

Clouds shot by, and the ground fell away. My stomach dropped to my feet. Eyes squeezed shut. Dizzy and sick, I leaned against Morrigan. Her heartbeat drummed in my ear. Sweet perfume smelling of rain and frost filled my nose. Soft, velvet-cloaked arms wrapped around me. The sick feeling vanished. I relaxed and opened my eyes.

Misty clouds, covered with a thin layer of icy frosting, floated below us. Diamond-tipped stars twinkled so bright and close that I reached out to grab them. Higher and higher we climbed then in one mighty swoop, dipped to skim inches above the ocean, our shadow reflected in the moonlit current. The cool spray of water stung my face like tiny frozen knives.

Excitement and joy bubbled deep in my chest until I let out a yell. Had to or bust.

Castles loomed below us. "Scotland," Morrigan whispered. "Home."

Pyramids rose from the sand in Egypt, snow-covered mountains in Tibet threw iced air against my skin. On and on we flew until the grass of the hollow's clearing rose up to greet us.

Cool, soft lips brushed my forehead, and Morrigan sent a smile straight into my soul, searing it forever.

"Happy Halloween, James Logan."

I woke up snuggled deep into my blankets. Had it been a dream? No. It was too real. My hand brushed against something soft. Lying beside me was a dark leather pouch. Wiping sleep from my eyes, I pulled the drawstrings open and unfolded the parchment inside.

"Only the brave and noble are worthy enough to fly with a warrior witch. I will return again on All Hollow's Eve. Watch for me."

Things changed fast after that night.

First, and most important, Mom got engaged. She had a flat tire coming home from work.

"And a stranger appeared out of nowhere to change it," she gushed. "His name is Alan Goodman and he reminds me so much of your father."

Flying with a witch made me forget all about the love spell. True to Morrigan's word, when I quit thinking about him, "A. Goodman" showed up.

Second, Loony Lonnie stopped hitting me. I caught his fist in my bare hand and curled my fingers around it.

"No!"

"Ever since Halloween, you've been different," Butch said. "Not such a scaredy-cat. What happened to you?"

I arched only my right eyebrow and shrugged. Never told him. That night would forever remain a sacred secret between the Witch of Moon Hollow and me.

A calendar with a picture of a black Ford Mustang convertible hangs above my bed. Every night after Mom tucks me in, I scurry out from under the blankets and tear off that day's page.

My eyes close as I drift off into dreams where a winged horse paws the ground and waits for me. The wild wind carries Morrigan's laugh, and the scar deep in my soul burns.

Only five more days until Halloween.
Totally awesome!

ABOUT THE AUTHOR

R. H. Burkett, aka Ruth Weeks, is not only an award-winning author with five published books but is also an accomplished public speaker, contest judge, and writing instructor. Ruth served on the Board of Directors for Ozark Writers League as well. Her first novel, *Soldiers in the Mist,* was voted Ozark Writers League (OWL) 2012 Best Book of the Year. Her second novel, *Daughter of the Howling Moon,* was the Oklahoma Writers Federation's (OWFI) 2015 Book of the Year.

Raised in Fayetteville, Arkansas, she and her brother were the first set of boy/girl twins born at Washington Regional Hospital. Ruth attended the University of Arkansas, majoring in Drama. In addition to her writing, Weeks is also a professional international tarot card reader.